The Forge of
Darkness

ALSO BY SCOTT B. WILLIAMS

Fiction

The Pulse

Refuge

Voyage After the Collapse

The Darkness After

Into the River Lands

Sailing the Apocalypse

Nonfiction

On Island Time

Paddling the Pascagoula

Exploring Coastal Mississippi

Bug Out

Getting Out Alive:

ISBN-13: 978-1533197740
Cover photograph: © heshixin, file #95340774, fotolia
Cover and interior design: Scott B. Williams
Editor: Michelle Cleveland

The Forge of
Darkness

Darkness After Series

Scott B. Williams

For my good friend, Mike—a real Mississippi game warden doing a dangerous job

One

MITCH HENLEY IGNORED THE occasional drop of rain that splashed onto his forehead and face as he crouched there and watched. The dark clouds overhead muted the late afternoon light to a dreary gray that barely penetrated the dense river bottom forest, and Mitch knew the visibility would get worse as the rain picked up. This was the last chance to bring the day's hunt to a successful conclusion, and it was up to Jason to pull it off.

The small whitetail buck was slowly working its way along the top of the creek bank, and was probably 35 to 40 yards from where Jason was kneeling behind the flared base of a large cypress tree. Sensing the change in the weather, the animal was focused on its feeding, stopping only occasionally to raise its head and look for danger. But there was no breeze to carry the scent of man to its nostrils and the light rain helped to muffle any sound the three hunters might have inadvertently made. The soft "twang" of a bowstring released reached his ears and Mitch held his breath as he watched the flight of his friend's arrow streaking to its target. For him, this would be an easy shot; the kind he couldn't miss. But it was Jason's first attempt at a deer with the longbow. Mitch was glad to see him take the chance, because from where he watched, there was too much underbrush between him and the quarry for a shot of his own.

He grinned when he heard the satisfying "whack" of the arrow smacking flesh and saw the buck spin around and leap into the air just before it bounded off and disappeared into the gloom. Jason's arrow had certainly connected, but from his point of view, Mitch couldn't be sure where.

"It went too far to the right, dammit!" Jason said, when Mitch reached his side. "I think it hit him in the gut. It didn't even seem to hurt him from the way he took off!"

"Let's go see," Mitch said. "It probably did more damage than you think. Just because he ran off like that doesn't mean he'll get far. We'll be able to tell from the blood trail."

As the two of them walked to the spot where the deer had been standing, Jason's cousin, Corey joined them from where he'd been concealed near the bank even farther upstream.

"He ran right by me after Jason hit him and I got an arrow off, but didn't even touch him!" Corey said.

"That's not surprising, Corey. Not many people could hit a running deer with a bow, especially in thick woods on a rainy day like this when it's hard enough to even see a deer."

"You could," Jason said. "But you wouldn't have to because your first shot would have put him down."

"Not necessarily, but that's beside the point. You hit him, and we'll get him eventually. We'll just have to track him down. I think there's going to be enough blood to follow, see?"

Mitch pointed to the scattered droplets of crimson on the leaves of the forest floor. Like many of his recent hunts, his purpose today was to teach. Though he was happy doing the bulk of the hunting for the group by himself, he was pleased that some of the others were now working on their skills under his guidance. Jason and Corey had become eager students of the longbow and were ready to put what they'd learned into practice. He'd started them with the basics on the same target range behind the house where he'd mastered archery himself before taking to the woods to hunt live game. But there was no substitute for this real-world experience, and Mitch knew misses and botched shots were inevitable. Though he hated to see an animal suffer needlessly, he was confident they could track down the wounded buck and finish the job. Chances were it wouldn't run too far if they didn't push it too closely, but on the other hand, with the rain picking up, Mitch didn't want to risk losing the blood trail either.

They had just started moving, working from one splattering of blood to the next, when the faint crack of a rifle off in the far distance caused Mitch to pause. The sound came from the general direction of the farm, which was not entirely surprising, since there were no other human habitations within earshot of where they were. As he considered the possibilities, wondering who there might have fired it and why, two more closely spaced shots followed the first one, but some twenty or thirty seconds later.

"That was a high-powered rifle," Mitch said to Jason and Corey as the faint echoes died away.

"It must have been Tommy or David then, since they're usually on patrol this time of day. But what would they be shooting at?"

"That's what I'm wondering. The way the shots were spaced it sounded like someone hunting. Like maybe they missed or wounded whatever it was with the first shot and then followed up with that second and third one."

"Maybe one of them saw a deer too?" Corey suggested.

"Maybe, but I kind of doubt it. I guess it could have been a wild dog or some other varmint though."

Mitch knew that if a deer did appear while the others were occupied with something else, any one of them would take advantage of the opportunity to put meat on the table. But he didn't think that was likely, as there had been plenty of hunting pressure around the farm in the last few months, as well as a lot of other activity like gathering firewood in the nearby forest. Because of this, he did almost all of his hunting farther afield now, deep in the bottomlands here along the creek and beyond, and he didn't expect that situation to change.

Whatever the target, he was sure the rifle shots were fired

SCOTT B. WILLIAMS

for good reason if anyone from their group fired them. While they had conducted some practice and defensive drill sessions early on for the benefit of those among them with less shooting experience, wasting rifle ammunition was out of the question now. There was simply no telling how long they were going to have to make what they had last and no way of knowing when they were going to need a lot of it in a hurry to defend their lives and property. Hunting with the bow and arrow helped conserve what ammo they had for their various firearms. Fortunately, the materials for making more bows and arrows were readily available in the woods. Mitch at least, had the skills to utilize them, and he planned to teach the others over time.

Mitch had finally convinced the rest of them that thinking long-term was their best option. No one had any real answers about the bigger picture regarding their situation, but he could envision a scenario where the blackout lasted so long there wouldn't be other options. Aside from the issue of resupply, using bows rather than firearms enabled them to keep a lower profile. Rifle shots could be heard from a great distance, especially now that there were no other background sounds like faraway traffic or manmade machinery. Out here, any sound of human activity might attract the attention of strangers passing through the area. The last thing any of them wanted was to draw outsiders to the farm. Recent experience had shown that danger could approach not only from the gravel road that skirted the front of the property

11

but also by way of Black Creek. The creek was a natural travel corridor through the wild national forest lands in back of the Henley's 600-acre property. It could be followed on foot with some difficulty or easily navigated by canoe, and while useful to Mitch and everyone else living on the farm, it was potentially a backdoor standing wide open to unwanted guests.

Mitch and his two friends were within sight of Black Creek even as they heard the shots. The wounded buck's blood trail led upstream, even deeper into the forest and farther from the Henley farm. For a moment, Mitch considered whether they should turn back and head for home. But as he stood there, bow in hand, waiting and listening, there was only the sound of the steadily increasing rain pelting the leaves and the forest floor around them. The shooting was probably nothing significant, since there wasn't a follow-up or an answering exchange from a different weapon. Mitch wasn't really worried with Benny and Tommy around the house, and he knew April could hold her own too.

"Whatever it was, they must have gotten it," Jason said.

"Yeah, I don't think it's anything we need to worry about. Come on. Let's go find your deer. We don't have long before dark."

Two

THEY HAD JUST STARTED moving again when the rain increased to a downpour, the noise drowning out the possibility of hearing anything beyond the immediate vicinity, including more gunshots if there were any to be heard. It wasn't going to help that the rain would obliterate the blood trail they were trying to follow, but Mitch knew the area like the back of his hand. He had a pretty good idea where the wounded buck might go to lay up and hide, and they would find it eventually, if not by dark then first thing in the morning. The three of them were prepared to spend the night out if necessary, as it sometimes was on hunts like these. The others back at the house wouldn't be expecting them until they returned with meat, so no one would worry if they didn't show until tomorrow.

Mitch was doing his best not to worry either, but the sound of those rifle shots had made him uneasy, even if there was likely a good explanation for them. It was just that so much had happened since the grid went down that it was difficult for him to completely dismiss *anything* out of the ordinary. If it had sounded like more than one weapon being fired, he would have certainly headed back immediately. If Jason hadn't already wounded a deer they would have gone back anyway, as the heavier rain would have diminished the chances of a successful hunt. As he moved quickly, trying to find what traces of blood he could before the last of it washed away, he kept telling himself that all was fine back at the house. Benny was there, along with his son Tommy. Those two alone gave Mitch the confidence to stay away overnight. Mitch couldn't have hoped for a better pair to have around to help look out for the property and everyone there.

Things around the farm had just gotten back to a somewhat normal routine since the last encounter with outsiders led him into an unplanned adventure a few weeks prior. Harrowing as it was, that ordeal had turned out well in the end and had increased by five the number of survivors now living on the Henley place. More importantly, among those five were April Gibbs and her little daughter, Kimberly. Mitch had never expected to see the two of them again, but he'd never stopped thinking about April since that day he had said goodbye to her in Hattiesburg. He had doubted she still thought much about him, if at all, but then one day she had returned, making her way all the way out here by way of the creek. Mitch had been practically walking on air ever since.

Their time together in those first few days after the collapse had been brief, but filled with danger and excitement. Something had clicked between them, and the life or death battles they fought together forged a bond that couldn't be broken. April had come back, bringing both her little Kimberly, and Kimberly's father, David Green. Mitch wondered if David would suddenly snap out of his amnesia one day and remember their relationship, but even if he did, April said it wouldn't matter. She told him she had been through with David even before they left Hattiesburg. Now that she was back, Mitch was certain that the two of them were meant to be together; no matter how unlikely that had seemed when they had parted before.

She was on his mind now as he pushed through the wet undergrowth, the rain seemingly set in for the duration. It was going to be a long, miserable night if they had to camp in this, and a part of him wished that Jason hadn't made that shot after all. If not for the rain and the pressing darkness, he would have insisted that Jason do all the tracking, since it was his deer and that was the only way he was going to learn, but Mitch knew that would take a lot longer and he was impatient. He pushed on ahead, an arrow nocked on his bowstring, ready for a quick shot if the buck should bust out of cover and try to make another run for it.

Even when he wasn't on the trail of a wounded animal, Mitch kept an arrow ready on the string when he was in the woods. The practice had proven its worth countless times since the breakdown, and he had no intention of changing his ways anytime soon. In addition to his bow and the dozen hunting arrows carried in a buckskin quiver slung low and

THE FORGE OF DARKNESS

close to his side, his Ruger .357 Magnum rode in a holster on his belt. The revolver was there anytime he was dressed, from when he woke before dawn until he turned in for the night. All three of them were carrying firearms, even though they had no intention of using them for hunting. There was just no way of knowing who they might run into out here, so Mitch made it a point to keep everyone armed at all times. Jason had the AR-15 that was the state-issued patrol rifle Mitch's dad had kept in his truck. He was wearing it slung behind his back so that it wouldn't interfere with the use of the bow, but would be easy to bring into play if needed. Corey wore the Glock 10mm pistol that Benny had taken off the corpse of the man who'd abducted April. There were plenty of guns to go around for everyone; that wasn't the issue. The main limitation was the amount of ammo they had on hand for each. They were well stocked in some calibers like .22 Long Rifle and 5.56mm, but with so many different weapons among them, ammo for some of the handguns, rifles and shotguns was in short supply. Mitch hoped they had enough to make it last, especially if they had to continue defending the farm from outsiders finding their way into the area. Discussing this often with the others however, they all wondered how many survivors were actually left, as it had been nearly nine months since the collapse. Would those who were still hanging on keep to themselves, like his small group was doing? Or would they still be roaming the countryside, looking for others who had more than they, like the men who tried to take April and Kimberly?

Mitch and those living with him still didn't know if there was anywhere that was unaffected by the solar flares. They had to believe there must be, but how far away? No one they had met knew and everywhere in the region practically everything electronic or controlled by electronics was down. The result was far worse than a mere power outage though; the pulse had affected transportation and communication as well. In short, they were on their own, with bleak prospects of help or resupply. Most people, accustomed as they were to the comfort and conveniences of modern living, had fallen to pieces in the aftermath. Cut off and stranded, facing the prospect of individual responsibility for their survival for the first time in their lives; they found this new reality more than they could handle. Many were undoubtedly already dead. Those who remained were desperate; surely losing hope as the days, weeks and now months passed with no change in sight.

Mitch too, had been stranded in a world mostly alien to him on that first day. It was rare that he found himself in any city, but of all days that one when the solar flare hit was the one morning he had skipped school to drive his parents to the airport in New Orleans. After dropping them off, his father's brand new Ford F-150 stalled at an intersection along with hundreds of other vehicles crowding the streets in the morning rush. Mitch did the only thing he *could* do, and started walking out of the city. Fortunately, home was less than a hundred miles away to the northeast, in rural Mississippi. Mitch could get there in a matter of days and he had to, because his little sister was there alone until he returned.

There wasn't a day since that morning he set out that Mitch didn't think about his mom and dad. He had no way of knowing if they were alive or dead, but others in the streets had seen jet aircraft falling from the sky. The plumes of smoke in several places on the horizon confirmed it was true once he was out of the truck and talking to other drivers around him. Mitch had to assume that unless his parents' flight had already landed in Houston, they too were probably victims of a plane crash. There had been enough time for them to get there if the flight actually left when it was supposed to, but Mitch simply didn't know and he knew he never would unless they showed up at the farm one day. It was more than 400 miles from Houston to these south Mississippi woods, but if anyone could find a way to get back home, Mitch knew that Doug Henley could.

The skills and knowledge Mitch learned from his father were keeping him alive today. Mitch knew he was fortunate to have been raised the way he was and where. Out here in the backwoods, far from big cities and even small towns, his family had been largely self-sufficient even before the blackout. Mitch had learned to do many things the old way, including hunting and preserving foods. With more than two decades of outwitting poachers and other outlaws, his game warden father had seen it all and Mitch absorbed plenty listening to his tales of their mostly illegal tricks and methods. All of this backwoods knowledge was crucial now, and certainly would be more so the longer things went in the direction they were headed.

So while Mitch would have preferred to be back at the house, warm and dry and in the company of April rather than out here in the woods in the rain, the discomfort and inconvenience was nothing new to him. If they didn't find Jason's deer before dark, they would find a place to settle in for the evening and resume the search in the morning light. Next time Jason would be more careful with his aim. Mitch was sure of it.

Three

THE SUDDEN REPORT OF a high-powered rifle shattering the quiet of the piney woods stopped Benny Evans in his tracks. The shooter had to be close, probably within range of where he stood, but there had been no sound of a bullet impact and a quick check of the girls behind him reassured him they were both okay as well. The rain that had been falling for several minutes was enough to muffle smaller sounds, like people talking or moving through the woods, making the gunshot even more startling. Benny hadn't expected to encounter anyone out here, but it wasn't far to the dirt road that ran by the front of the Henley property. Tommy and David were out making their rounds of the perimeter, but they'd already passed this way and Benny and the girls had spoken with them as they worked their way to the back of the 600 acres. Tommy was carrying his .308, of course, and the shot Benny just heard could have come from a rifle like that, but it was in the wrong direction to be Tommy's. Besides that, his boy wouldn't be wasting ammo for no good reason. When two more shots followed the first, even as Benny contemplated this, he began to get concerned.

He quietly put down the axe he'd been carrying in one hand and reached for the Remington 12-gauge slung over his back. At the same time he turned and motioned for the girls to keep quiet and be still. They had been following just a few feet behind and were just as confused and startled by the sudden gunshots as he. Benny crouched to watch and listen, waiting for any sign of movement or other sounds out there among the pines. Just seconds later the silence was disturbed again. Something big was crashing through the brush ahead of him, from the direction in which the shots had come. Benny raised his shotgun and tensed as he strained to see through the screen of trees. Whatever it was, it was coming his way and making a lot of noise. Seconds passed and then he knew—*the cattle!* The small herd of brown and white Herefords was running right at him, busting their way through the woods in a panicked stampede. Benny backed up to where the girls were crouching and hurried them close to the base of the biggest nearby tree. The terrified herd split around them at the last minute, rushing past Benny and the girls on both sides. But just as he thought they were all gone, Benny noticed one of the yearling steers bringing up the rear, its gait hobbled by a useless leg. As it made its way past him, trying desperately to keep up with the rest of the herd, Benny saw the glistening blood that coated its hindquarters.

So that was it! Someone had shot at Doug Henley's cattle! Until he saw the wounded animal, Benny hadn't realized what had happened, so he hadn't thought to try and get a count of the animals running by. But there had been three shots. Unless the other two missed, there could be cattle down in addition to this one that was obviously wounded. *Mitch was going to be furious when he found out about this!*

"Lisa, you and Stacy need to get back to the house! Tell April and Samantha there's a trespasser out here somewhere and that y'all need to stay inside and keep the doors locked."

"We can't leave you out here alone, Uncle Benny," Lisa said. "Just because it was one person doing the shooting doesn't mean there aren't more. April and the others would have heard it anyway, and Tommy knows we don't have a rifle with us. I'll bet he and David are headed back this way already. We can sneak up there with you and see who it is in the meantime, and help you make sure they don't get away."

Benny considered what Lisa said and figured it made sense. Mitch Henley's little sister was a brave one, and she and Stacy had both seen their share of violence since things fell apart. He didn't want to put them at any unnecessary risk, but he knew they could both be quiet and it wouldn't hurt to find out more before he sent them back to warn April. There was no use raising a major alarm if it was just one or two desperate wanderers passing through that took a shot at the cattle because the opportunity presented itself. They could slip up close enough to see who had done it and size them up without being seen. Benny was sure that was the way Mitch would handle this if he were here, and once he had an idea who he was dealing with he would take the appropriate action to make them wish they'd never seen those cows. It was hard enough looking after the livestock without worrying about some low-life rustler shooting it for meat.

So far, the small herd of just over two dozen animals had survived and had stayed within the fence. Mitch and Jason had expanded it since the collapse, using all the barbed wire on hand and cutting their own posts, so that it now followed the boundaries of the entire property. The expansion allowed the cattle to range from the bottomlands near the creek to the more open woods and pastures, and would help stretch what little leftover hay and feed there was in the barn through another winter. Most of the time the herd stayed out of sight of the house and yard, now that they were foraging more. But Mitch wanted to keep them around and keep them alive as long as possible, because with as many people as they had staying on the farm now, he knew the time would come when finding enough deer and other game close enough to home would become difficult. Beef would have to be slaughtered, and he hoped to put it off a lot longer, but Benny agreed that it was inevitable.

* * *

Benny hadn't been thinking about the cattle at all though until he heard the shots and saw the stampeding herd. His quest today with Lisa and Stacy was far more important. It had brought the three of them out to the edge of the property near the road because there were a few Eastern red cedars mixed in among the pines growing there. But just before all the unexpected commotion, Benny had been about ready to call off their search for the day and go back home. Heavier rain was coming, and it was getting late. He'd told the girls they probably wouldn't find the tree they were looking for until tomorrow, even though Stacy was sure they already had a half hour earlier:

"This one is the perfect shape! Look at how even it is all the way around!"

Benny had just laughed. "We couldn't even get that one through the door without cutting it half in two! And that's if we could even drag it back to the house. That thing's nearly fifteen feet tall!"

"But it's *so* pretty!"

"Yeah, but it *is* big, Stacy," Lisa said. "I think Uncle Benny's right. It probably won't fit."

"I *know* it won't fit," Benny said. "The ceilings in that house ain't but eight feet high. Besides that, the doorway's only three feet wide and that thing's got a spread of seven or eight feet at the base! We'll find a smaller one just like it. We just gotta keep looking."

It was a pretty cedar all right, shaped just the way a Christmas tree was supposed to be, but it was simply too big to work. Looking for a Christmas tree was about the last thing Benny Evans ever expected to be doing again, especially after everything that happened in the last few months. Even before, when Betsy was still alive, the two of them had stopped making a fuss over holiday decorations. Betsy had a small artificial tree they still set up in front of the living room window every year, along with a plastic holly wreath they hung on the door, but that was about it. He couldn't recall how many years it had been since he'd last cut down a live cedar for a Christmas tree, but he figured it was when Tommy was a young boy, certainly no older than these two fourteen-year-old girls. Tommy was forty now, so that had been a little while. Regardless of that, Benny was just delighted that the girls wanted to spend time with him and that they both were already calling him "Uncle Benny" even though he'd only known them a few weeks.

Benny still couldn't believe the good fortune that had befallen him and his son since the day he'd found April Gibbs and her child tied up in that canoe under a steep bank on Black Creek. The man who'd left them that way had tried to kill his boy with an arrow, but his aim had been off enough that the broadhead cut through Tommy's upper arm instead of the middle of his back. Benny had sent that bastard straight to hell with a blast of double-aught buck from his 12-gauge, but it had been a real close call. Now, thanks to April, he and Tommy practically had a new family along with a real place to call home. Benny was a woodsman at heart and had taught his boy all he knew, but living out of a canoe for seven months straight, always on the move and always in hiding in the deep woods had gotten pretty old. The truth was, Benny himself had gotten older than he wanted to admit. He was doing okay for nearly 70, but living outside like that was hard, even on a young man. Things were a lot easier here on the Henley farm, even if they *were* still harder than life before all this happened.

Benny was mighty grateful that Mitch had agreed to take him and Tommy in, but Mitch had assured him he was just as thankful for what they'd done for April. Despite all that, Benny and Tommy both were determined to earn their keep around the place. And today, that meant finding whoever had fired those rifle shots and making sure they didn't do anything else to threaten the security of everyone living there. He whispered a last warning to Lisa and Stacy before they got started:

"I want you both to stay back several yards behind me while we're sneaking up there. If you see me stop, you stop! Don't move, don't talk and don't do nothin' until I do." Benny knew the girls would follow his orders. They knew how to be quiet, and the soft rain would help, making stalking the shooter even easier. He handed Stacy the axe he'd been carrying so that he would have both hands free for his shotgun. Lisa had her own weapon—the Ruger 10/22 that she'd already been a crack shot with even before the collapse. Benny gave them both a reassuring thumbs-up and then he started working his way through the pines.

Four

THE SHOOTER IGNORED THE soft rain, focusing all his attention on his target as he centered the crosshairs of his riflescope behind the shoulder of the nearest of the grazing steers. The butt stock of the 30.06 slammed into his shoulder with its familiar punch and he smiled as he saw the unsuspecting animal go down—hundreds of pounds of meat secured with a single bullet! He opened the bolt to eject the spent case and slid it home to chamber another round, scanning the rest of the small herd to pick his next target while he still had the chance. The remaining animals were startled and disoriented, unsure what to make of the sudden rifle blast and the sight of one of their number thrashing about on the ground, kicking out its death spasms. They would probably panic and bolt at the next shot, so he had to make it count. Picking another steer about the same size as the first, the shooter squeezed off his second round and saw his target fall, then he rapidly racked the bolt again as sure enough, the rest of the herd turned to run into the cover of the woods. He took quick aim and fired again, hitting one of the yearlings and seeing it stagger but keep going. The bullet missed its vitals, striking the hindquarters instead because it was already running away. Before he could get a forth round in the chamber, the cattle were out of sight, but it didn't matter. Two were down and the rest wouldn't go far, judging by the quality of the fence, at least what he could see of it. They could be rounded up tomorrow or the day after. Tonight there would be a feast and when the rest of the herd was corralled, there would be enough to feed everyone for a good long while.

The shooter knew that a herd of cattle like this in one place inside a fence that was in good repair meant someone was still around to take care of them. There would be a house somewhere nearby, he was sure of that. Someone would lay claim the cattle, whether they were the original owners still hanging on here or simply wanderers who had taken up residence since the collapse, but it wouldn't matter. Whoever they were, there would not be enough of them to resist. No one they'd encountered so far had been able to. That's why he had no fear of his shots being heard and had acted to secure meat immediately while the opportunity was there. There were a lot of mouths to feed and they had been on the move for too long. What happened next would be dealt with as necessary. He turned to the boy who was lying on the ground beside him.

"Run back there and tell Mr. Drake and the rest of them what we got! Tell him to bring the horses and get on down here before it gets dark. Tell him to send somebody back to tell everybody else too, because we've found us a new place to call home for a while!"

The boy took off immediately, knowing better than to hesitate or question a direct order from his father. It wouldn't take him long to get to where Drake and the others were waiting. They were on the road not far behind, just holding back a bit for the scouts to reconnoiter on foot. The rest were a couple of days back, traveling much slower because of the women and little kids and all of their stuff. It was always like this when they moved somewhere—the hunters and scouts going far ahead, checking things out and making sure the way was clear—and the rest of the community following, but not too closely.

The shooter watched the boy go until he was out of sight. Then he turned and with a wave of his hand signaled his eldest boy, Kenny, to move in and secure the kills. The tall, lanky teenager rose from where he'd been hiding on the hillside behind his father, and made his way down to the gravel road, stepping across only after making sure it was still empty. The shooter stayed put, remaining in the prone position from which he'd made his shots, the rifle still covering the lifeless animals he'd put down. He figured Drake and the other men would get there with the horses before whoever lived around here showed up, but he wasn't taking any chances until they did.

31

THE FORGE OF DARKNESS

* * *

April Gibbs stood at the sound of the second two rifle shots. She had been sitting in the rocking chair in the living room of the Henley house with Kimberly asleep in her arms. The first shot that seemed to come from out front, in the direction of the road, caused her to stop rocking and ponder who fired it. But when two more followed, she began to really wonder. It had to have been Tommy if it was anyone from among her friends. Benny and the girls were out there somewhere, but they didn't have a high-powered rifle. Benny's weapon of choice was the 12-gauge shotgun he'd been carrying the day she'd met him, and Lisa had her trusty .22 carbine, as always. But they wouldn't be shooting while out looking for a Christmas tree anyway, and neither would Tommy or David, who were on patrol—unless there was a really good reason.

April carried her daughter into the bedroom and placed her gently in the baby bed Mitch had pulled down from the attic where his parents had stashed it when Lisa had outgrown it. She waited a moment, watching Kimberly to make sure she didn't wake before leaving her, then grabbed her carbine and opened the door to the front porch. A light rain was falling, and the sky had gotten darker than it should be at that hour, indicating the weather wasn't going to get any better. She was sure Tommy had probably fired those shots, but at what? *Maybe he had seen a deer while he and David were making their rounds?* She was sure it was something like that, but after all she'd been through, she couldn't help but be nervous.

The few short weeks since she and Kimberly and David had arrived here at the farm were really the only time since the lights went out that she'd not felt like she was living with the constant threat of another attack. Most of the time it felt safe here, especially when Mitch was at home, but she knew the others added to their security too. Like Mitch, Benny and Tommy were competent woodsmen before the collapse, and Jason was learning fast, as was his cousin, Cory, who had arrived long before April with his girlfriend, Samantha. Lisa and Stacy, Mitch and Jason's little sisters, could do their share too, even if they *were* only fourteen. If there was anyone in their group they couldn't really count on for much, it was David Greene, April's former fiancé and father of her child.

April had been done with him as a partner even before their journey down Black Creek to seek out Mitch, but she couldn't abandon him entirely, for Kimberly's sake. The attack on the sandbar where he was left for dead had in some ways made her life easier, because David no longer knew who he was, let alone April. The sad part of that though was that he didn't remember his child either. Little Kimberly still called him "daddy," and he went along with it, believing that she had lost her real daddy and mistakenly thought he was her father. When he'd questioned April about this, she'd agreed, saying that must be it, because he looked a lot like her father. It was a lie, but it satisfied him and solved the problem of further confusing their child. April didn't know if David would eventually regain his memory and recognize the two of them or not, but she would deal with that when the time came, if it ever did. But at least he was alive, and lucky to be so, thanks to Mitch. She had to admit he was making himself more useful now that he didn't know who he was. It was good to see he seemed to have forgotten his former obnoxious, self-entitled attitude that had made it so difficult for him to adapt in those first months after the blackout. Now, with his new personality, living entirely in the present moment, he was showing some interest in learning how to survive in this harsh new reality, and was cooperating and at least trying to do his share. Maybe there was hope for him after all...

April stepped off the porch walked around to the backyard to the shed attached to the barn, where she knew Samantha was busy scraping deer hides.

"Did those shots sound to you like they came from out by the road?"

"I think so," Samantha said. "I figured it was Tommy shooting at something. I didn't hear anything else."

"You haven't seen Benny and the girls?"

"No. They must not have found a tree yet. I figured they would come back when it started raining."

"I'm sure Benny would have, but knowing Lisa and Stacy, they probably won't let him turn around until they get the tree they want."

"Probably not. I sure hope Corey and the guys got lucky and can come back tonight. I'd hate for them to have to camp in weather like this."

"Knowing Mitch, he's probably gotten them far enough from home that they'll have to. It's all part of the fun for him, and his way of testing Jason and Corey."

"I know, right? Guys are so weird. We already know they're badass. They don't have anything to prove at this point, but they'll keep doing it anyway."

"No doubt about that! Well, hopefully Tommy and David will be back soon. I'm curious to know what that shooting was about. I'm going back in to make sure Kimberly is still asleep. If you hear anything else usual, come get me."

Five

TOMMY EVANS HAD STARTED his day cutting and splitting firewood, like he did every day. If there was one downside to living on the Henley Farm, it was the routine chores that were never done, always the same, over and over, day after day. When Tommy and his daddy were living out of the canoe, ranging up and down Black Creek as needed to find enough game, he'd had to gather firewood too, but not on a scale anything like this. Camping on the creek bank and moving often, enough driftwood and fat lighter knot could be found on the sandbars and in the nearby woods to meet the needs of the two of them with minimal effort. Tommy and his daddy had shared the modest workload, each of them paddling and poling the canoe, setting up and striking camp, hunting and butchering game, and building the cooking fires. But here on the farm, things were different. With so many people living in one house in a fixed location, chores like wood gathering and splitting needed to be delegated and shared among them. Tommy still went hunting once in a while, but he and his daddy both had a hard time keeping up with Mitch and the other young guys, who were now ranging farther and farther afield in the pursuit of whitetail deer. So with the choice between endless miles of walking and packing home meat, or staying home and doing chores, Tommy usually picked the chores.

He still got his share of walking most days, even if it wasn't as far. After Mitch Henley had returned, shortly after Tommy and Benny first got there with April, there had been many discussions about security. It was impossible to watch over the entire 600-acres of woods and pasture twenty-four seven, but after the encounter with the men who'd taken April and Kimberly captive, Mitch said they had to do more. And since there were now more of them among which to divide the duties, it was decided that someone should make the rounds at least once a day, roughly following the perimeter of the property. Doing this would increase their chances of spotting any unusual activity or signs of trespassers, while also keeping a check on the gates and the barbed-wire fences that bounded the property. They couldn't watch every part of the perimeter at all times, of course, but it was better than doing nothing. Tommy liked this duty much better than cutting wood, and he looked forward to making the rounds each afternoon, usually at a leisurely pace.

Today, like most days, he had David Green tagging along. When Tommy had first met David he looked like he'd been wallowing around in the mud for days. His hair and bare feet were caked with it and his clothes were filthy and torn. He

38

had a wild look about him and didn't seem to know what to do or how to act when Mitch first brought him to the house. Tommy had been shocked to learn soon after that David Green had actually been April's fiancé before the lights went out and that he was the father of her little girl. David didn't know any of this though; because he'd been hit so hard in the head he didn't remember anything about his past.

Tommy figured that was probably a good thing too because it quickly became pretty obvious that April was more interested in Mitch Henley than David Green, even if she did have a kid with him. It was also pretty obvious that Mitch was just as infatuated with her, and Tommy sure couldn't blame him. It was all he could do to keep his eyes off her ever since that first day he'd met her down on the creek. April was one of the prettiest girls Tommy had ever seen, and not only was she pretty; she was tough too. He saw that real quick with the way she carried herself in the woods and also around the farm after they got there. Tommy knew all he could do was dream about having a girl like April though. She'd never take an interest in a shy 40-year-old country boy that had always been nervous around pretty girls and women. Tommy had never even had a real girlfriend and he had certainly never been married. He hoped he would one day, but with the way things were, it seemed less likely than before. But sometimes when he was making the rounds, especially out by the road, he daydreamed about finding another girl like April—but one that was lost, alone and afraid, and looking for a place to stay and someone to protect her. Tommy was sure that if he found a girl like that she would agree to marry him, because things were different now and the things he knew how to do like hunting and chopping wood were useful.

This had been on his mind again today, interrupted briefly when he and David ran into Benny and the two kids out looking for a Christmas tree. After talking with them for a few minutes, he was on his way again, slipping back into his daydreams as David followed close behind, carrying the long sharpened stick he'd fashioned into a spear. David acted like a little kid in some ways, always wanting to play games or pretend, and Tommy knew it was because he didn't know where he was or even who he was. With no concept of the past, he didn't know things were different now than they had always been, and having nothing to compare it to, he had no grasp of or worry of the future either. David Green was living in the moment, just as happy as he could be most of the time, no matter what they were doing. Tommy figured if carrying a spear made him feel good, then that was all right too. He probably didn't have any business toting a gun and besides, Tommy felt like he could handle any situation they might encounter right by himself with his trusty .308.

They were headed down the path that led to the back of the property, near the creek, when Tommy heard the first rifle shot. There was no doubt in his mind where it came from— somewhere back from the way they'd just come—out in the direction of the road. Tommy knew his daddy didn't have a rifle with him. He'd just seen him and like always, he had that 12-gauge pump slung across his back. Mitch's little sister had her .22, but what Tommy just heard was no .22. When two more shots followed a few seconds later, Tommy knew what he had to do.

"Come on, David. We've got to get back up to the road and see what that's all about!"

* * *

Benny Evans took great care as he slipped his way through the pines in the direction from which Doug Henley's cattle had stampeded. He was almost certain that whoever it was who'd done the shooting was an outsider not from around these parts. Benny doubted anyone who knew who the legendary game warden was would have the nerve to shoot his cattle. Benny had never met Doug Henley himself, but everyone in this part of Mississippi knew of him— especially anyone that did any hunting or fishing. No one wanted to run afoul of the game laws around here because there wasn't any getting away with it with Doug Henley around.

And while he might not be around now and might never come back, his boy Mitch was no doubt made from the same mold and Benny was mighty impressed with him. It didn't matter that he was still just a teenager; Mitch Henley was the best hunter Benny Evans had ever run across, and he'd known plenty of fine woodsmen in his day. The boy was simply a natural and his skill with that wooden longbow was a sight to behold. Whoever it was who'd made the mistake of shooting into that precious herd was going to regret it, Benny was sure of that. Benny might get there first, but Mitch would be along eventually, even if it were tomorrow. Benny just hoped whoever it was; he didn't try to get belligerent about it. He'd hate to have to kill another man so soon, but he was prepared to if it came down to it.

When he knew he was almost within sight of the gravel road, Benny stopped and stood motionless, watching and listening. He knew Lisa and Stacy were doing the same; he didn't even have to glance back to make sure. The rain had picked up a bit, still not much more than a light shower, but enough that it not only would have muffled any sound of their approach, but also the movements of whoever it was he expected to find here. Benny knew he had to be cautious, because anyone brazen enough to shoot another man's livestock inside a property fence probably wouldn't hesitate to shoot him too. When nothing stirred in the small area he could see through the trees, he took a few steps forward and stopped again to look and listen. After repeating this twice more, Benny finally saw what he'd expected to find.

Two of Doug Henley's cattle were lying on in the grass near the fence, just twenty or so yards from the gravel road. A tall figure wearing brown work coveralls emerged from the trees on the other side of the road and crossed it quickly.

Benny saw that he was carrying a hunting rifle of some kind, but he couldn't tell what it was. Benny watched as he bent and stepped through the barbed wire strands and onto the property, then leaned his weapon against a tree near the dead animals and drew a large skinning knife from his belt. He appeared to be alone, but Benny watched to be sure. After waiting several minutes, he glanced back at the girls so they could read his lips, as he silently impressed upon them that they were to absolutely stay put no matter *what* happened. When he was assured that they understood by the solemn nods he got from both of them, Benny turned his attention back to the intruder. Keeping his shotgun leveled and his finger on the trigger, Benny crept closer, knowing the rain would cover any sounds he might make and that his movement would go unnoticed as the cattle rustler focused on his bloody task.

Six

TOMMY EVANS KNEW WITHOUT a doubt that whoever fired those rifle shots was an outsider. It couldn't have been his daddy or Lisa or Stacy, and it sure wasn't Mitch or the other guys, because they were hunting way off down in the bottomlands and they would use their bows and arrows anyway. He figured he'd better hurry, because his daddy and the girls were up that way, probably pretty close to whoever it was. He knew a shortcut to get to the road without retracing the route they had taken on their patrol, and he walked as fast as he could without running, David following right behind him.

When he came within sight of the road, he slowed his pace, as he was quite sure it was the road that must have brought the intruder to the area in the first place. He turned to follow it, keeping in the woods inside the fence on the hidden path that was their normal route used when patrolling the property. He figured if he followed it far enough, it would lead him to whoever fired those shots, but he sure didn't want to be seen until he and David saw them first. Why anyone passing through would be shooting, Tommy didn't know. He just hoped it didn't involve his daddy or those girls. With it raining like it was now, he hoped they'd gone back to the house and given up on finding a Christmas tree today anyway.

He glanced back at David and whispered to him how important it was that they keep quiet. He thought he could trust him to stay back and keep his mouth shut, but it made him nervous. David seemed to get it, though. He was creeping along, watching ever step Tommy took and trying to copy his movements. And he had that silly sharpened stick in his hands, poised like a spear ready to thrust at any danger that might appear. Tommy certainly didn't intend for them to encounter anything that close range though. With the .308 in his hands he didn't figure they'd have to.

He had just about reached the corner of the Henley property where the fence turned away from the road again when he saw someone step out of the woods. Tommy stopped in his tracks and squinted through the rain. Whoever it was, he was crossing the road and walking onto Henley land, and he was carrying a gun. Tommy figured he had to be the mystery shooter. He watched to see what the stranger was up to, and that's when he saw something brown and white, lying in the low grass and undergrowth just inside the fence up ahead. It took him a few seconds to register what it was, and then he knew—it was one of the cattle—and it was dead! He bent down so he could see better under the low hanging pine branches and then saw that there was another one nearby too. The stranger leaned his rifle against a tree and pulled out a knife. Then he knelt down in front of one of the dead animals, clearly getting ready to cut its throat and bleed it. *So that was it! That's what the shooting was all about, killing Mitch's cattle for their meat!*

Tommy turned to David and told him to stay right where he was and keep his mouth shut. Then he started down the path at a brisk pace, his anger building as he closed in on the stranger, who had his back turned to him. When he was within twenty paces, he stopped:

"HEY! WHAT DO YOU THINK YOU'RE DOING?"

The stranger turned to face him, clearly startled by his sudden appearance, and Tommy saw that he couldn't have been much older than about fifteen or sixteen. He had gotten to his feet and still had the knife in his hand, unfazed by the rifle Tommy was pointing at him. Tommy was about to tell him to drop the knife but before he could utter the words the sharpest pain he'd ever felt slammed into his side, burning through him like a hot needle and taking his breath away. He was aware of the rifle slipping out of his hands as his knees buckled beneath him and then his next sensation was that of his face pressed against the wet pine needles that covered the ground. Tommy didn't understand what had just happened. He knew he needed to get back up, but his body wouldn't do what his mind willed it to.

* * *

THE FORGE OF DARKNESS

The shooter cursed under his breath as he watched his son kneel beside the first steer, so intent on what he was doing that he was oblivious to his surroundings. It was a good thing he'd decided to stay put and keep watch. He knew someone had to be looking after any cattle that still looked that good, but he hadn't really expected them to show up so fast. When he noticed movement in the trees just inside the fence line, he wished there was some way he could warn Kenny that he was not alone, but it would be impossible without giving away his position and losing the advantage he had by remaining unseen. He tried to get his crosshairs on the man as he approached, but there were too many branches in the way, so he waited, tracking his movement as best he could until he finally stopped. Unbelievably, that stupid teen-aged boy of his still didn't know he had been seen until the man said something to him. From his position across the road, the shooter couldn't hear what it was, but he saw that the man was carrying a rifle and that he was holding it at hip level, the muzzle pointed in his son's direction. It didn't look like he was going to shoot him immediately, but when Kenny turned to face him, standing up with the knife still in his hand; he decided it wasn't worth waiting to find out. The man was in the open now and he had a clear shot, so he put his crosshairs on him and squeezed the trigger, dropping him instantly. His son glanced over his way for a second at the sound of the rifle, but then turned to face something else—another man running at him from the same general area the first one had come from. He ran with one hand raised overhead, poised as if to throw something.

The shooter saw what looked like a long stick fly past Kenny's head as he tried to get lined up on this new target. It missed him clean and stuck in the ground several yards farther back, and he realized it was a spear. At least his kid wasn't backing down, and he smiled when he saw him close in on the screaming stranger with his knife. Since the other man appeared to be unarmed but for the stick he'd already thrown, the shooter decided he would let Kenny take him with the knife. It wouldn't be his first, and it was what he would surely want to do to save face after being dumb enough to let a couple of farmers get the drop on him like that. The shooter thought it would be fun to watch and he was sure of the outcome; but then from out of nowhere, there was another gunshot that came as a total surprise. He saw his son collapse into a heap, his knife landing on the ground beside him. Kenny wasn't moving and was probably dead before he realized he had been shot!

* * *

Benny had closed half the distance to the unsuspecting trespasser when all of a sudden he heard a shout. The voice came from somewhere among the trees off to his left, closer to the road, and he could have sworn it sounded like his boy,

Tommy. But Benny couldn't see anyone. The stranger got up and turned to face whoever it was, and for the first time, Benny got a good look at his face. He was young, just a boy really, but when he stood up he was brandishing that bloody knife like he wasn't afraid of anything. Benny knew the boy wasn't aware of his presence; his focus was completely on what had startled him.

Benny eased closer, to try and get to where he could see for himself who it was, when all of a sudden another rifle shot boomed out from somewhere across the road. So there *was* more than one of them! Benny had been right to be suspicious that there would be, but whoever he or she was, the shooter had not been aiming at him. A chill swept over him as he thought about Tommy again. Could that have really been his voice? Benny had to get close enough to find out, but he couldn't risk being seen, either by the boy he was stalking or the unseen shooter across the road.

The sound of the rifle caused the trespasser with the knife to turn and glance at the wooded hillside where Benny was sure the shot had come from. But then he turned his attention in the direction from which he'd been surprised when he first stood. Ignoring the rifle leaning against the tree, he held the knife like he was getting ready to use it and began advancing. Benny glanced back to where the girls were hiding, signaling with a subtle motion of his hand that they were to stay put. Then, just as he turned his attention back to the scene unfolding before him, he was startled by a wild scream of rage.

He saw a flash of movement among the pines, and then he recognized David, who he knew had been with Tommy earlier. David was running right at the stranger with the knife, his crude wooden spear poised to throw. When he did throw it, Benny saw it miss completely, sailing right past the boy with the knife, who didn't seem to care. Instead he just laughed and stepped closer to David, waving the big blade in a way that left no doubt as to what he intended to do with it. Benny moved in to intervene, but the boy was focused on David and oblivious to his approach. From where he stood now, Benny could see someone lying on the ground between David and the stranger. He couldn't see his face, the way he was sprawled on the ground, but he could see what he was wearing, and the rifle that was lying there beside him, and that was enough: *It was Tommy! The rifle shot he'd just heard was someone shooting Tommy, and now this boy was about to stab David!*

Benny raised his shotgun to his shoulder and drew a bead on the stranger's chest. When the boy took his next step in David's direction, it was his last. Benny let him have it center of mass with a round of double aught buck.

Seven

THE RIFLE FROM ACROSS the road rang out again as Benny crawled closer to where David was bent over the prostrate body that Benny knew was his boy. Benny saw a bullet kick up dirt just beyond where it skimmed over David's head, and knew the next one probably wouldn't miss.

"David! Grab Tommy's rifle and get over here and get down behind these trees before you get yourself killed! How bad is Tommy hit?" But Benny already knew the answer before he asked. The rifle that had put down those 800-pound steers with one shot each would certainly be lethal to a man if it was a solid hit. Seeing his boy lying there, he feared the worst already.

David did as he was told and scrambled on his knees and elbows to the cluster of trees where Benny was now crouching, another bullet just missing him before he reached safe cover. "He won't move Benny! I told him he needed to get up and get over here, but he wouldn't do anything!"

"Is he still breathing? Could you tell if he could hear you or not?" Benny had to find out, but with that rifle over there

THE FORGE OF DARKNESS

across the road, it would be suicide to try. He glanced at the body of the one that he'd shot, the one who'd threatened David with the knife. That one sure wasn't going to hurt anybody. He'd been dead before he hit the ground. Benny checked the magazine of Tommy's .308. It was full but for the one round Tommy had already chambered. That left four more to follow-up. Five rounds wasn't much but Benny knew the extra reach of a rifle over his shotgun would be helpful in this situation. He eyed the weapon the dead boy had left leaning against a tree over by the steers. It looked like an older semi-automatic hunting rifle, maybe a .308 as well or perhaps a .243 or something. Benny figured it might come in handy as a back up to Tommy's rifle and his shotgun if they could get their hands on it without getting shot. Whatever it took, he aimed to get that bastard over there across the road that had shot his boy. But first he had to get Tommy moved behind these trees and see if he was even still alive. To do that he had to somehow draw fire from the shooter and try and figure out where he was. And he needed that other rifle so they would have enough ammo to keep him busy while one of them went to get Tommy.

"I'm gonna make a run for that rifle over there by them carcasses," he told David, handing him the shotgun. "As soon as he takes a shot at me, you shoot a couple rounds of that buckshot up there to keep him ducking."

"What if he hits you with his first shot?"

"Let's hope he won't. I don't plan on making it easy for

him."

Benny was just about to make his run for it when he suddenly heard bodies crashing into the leaves behind him and realized Lisa and Stacy were there, diving for cover with him and David. They had run there from where he'd left them, Lisa with her 10/22 carbine in her hands and Stacy still carrying the axe.

"What are you two doing? I told you to stay put!"

"We couldn't stay back there with all this shooting going on," Lisa said. "It sounded like you needed help." She looked at David. "Where's Tommy?"

"He's been shot, Lisa!" Benny said. "I've got to get him over here without getting shot myself in the process."

Lisa looked to where Benny pointed and saw Tommy lying there. As she did, gasping in shock, Benny glanced at her little 10/22 and got an idea. It had a 30-round magazine and it was a semi-automatic. It might have only a fraction of the stopping power of their adversary's weapon, but rapid firepower would come in handy for what he had in mind.

"Listen here, Lisa. If you want to help, here's what you can do. When David and I get ready to go and I give the word, you open up with your rifle and keep up a steady rate of fire against that hillside; not too fast, but just steady. We don't know exactly where that feller is, but if you just keep shooting that way maybe you can keep his head down so he can't shoot us. We'll run out there and drag Tommy back over here just as fast as we can. Do you think you can do that?"

"Of course I can, Uncle Benny. But wouldn't it be better if you did the shooting and the three of us went to get Tommy?"

"I might be old, young lady, but I'm plenty fast enough when I need to be. And besides, if anyone else is gonna get shot trying to get my boy back, it ought to be me. I hate for David to take the risk too but I am *not* going to put you two in that kind of danger. I ain't planning to get shot though because I've got to get Tommy and then I got a feller to hunt down just as soon as I do! Now let's not waste anymore time! David, I'm ready to go when you are!"

* * *

Lisa Henley tried to spot anything that looked like a person hiding on the wooded slope across the road, but nothing moved. She aimed her rifle at a stump for the first round and figured she would just shoot randomly all around the area and hope she was getting close. Like Uncle Benny said, at least if whoever it was over there thought he was under fire, maybe he would keep his head down and not try to shoot back at the same time.

When Benny said 'Go!' Lisa pulled the trigger and methodically fired round after round as she saw him and David out of the corner of her eye, scrambling low until they got to either side of Tommy and reached down to grab him under his arms. Lisa knew it was up to her to keep them

SCOTT B. WILLIAMS

covered, so she kept firing, trying to pace it so that she wouldn't empty the magazine before they had Tommy back. The two of them worked quickly so it only took a few seconds. When they were back behind the trees, Lisa stopped shooting and turned to look at Tommy.

What she saw was horrible. Poor Tommy's wool shirt was completely soaked with blood and he was trying to say something but couldn't seem to even breathe well, much less talk. Uncle Benny was bent over him, trying to wipe away the blood to find his wound and stop him from bleeding to death. David was looking on, wide-eyed and confused, completely at a loss as to what to do. He and Uncle Benny both had bloody hands from moving Tommy, and it looked to Lisa like there was so much blood poor Tommy was bound to die. She glanced back at the empty woods across the road, wondering where the awful person who shot him was now. She wished she could see him to get a clear shot, but there had been no return fire either during or after her fusillade of bullets. She glanced at the clear plastic magazine and saw that she still had two rounds left. She had fired 23 in all then. She removed the magazine and began reloading it from the stash of loose rounds she carried in the pocket of her jeans.

"Lisa, you and Stacy need to get back to the house right now," Uncle Benny said. "You get back there and tell April and Samantha what happened and get that wheeled firewood travois we built and pull it out here. We've got to get Tommy back to the house but we've got to move him gently. Rolling

57

him back on that thing is the best way I know to do it."

"But what about that other stranger that's still out there, Uncle Benny? He could still be waiting for a chance to shoot you and David too. He might come over here."

"I think whoever shot Tommy is probably trying to get away right now. With all your shooting on top of me killing his partner, he probably figured he was outnumbered and high-tailed it. But I aim to catch him before he gets far. I'm the only one that can do it and I don't think it will take long. David can stay here with Tommy until I get back, or if y'all get back first, go ahead and move him to the house. Don't wait for me. Now go!"

Lisa had never seen Uncle Benny look so serious. His eyes were practically burning with fury, and she understood his rage. Although she hated for him to go alone, what he said made sense. They needed to get Tommy to the house where they could see what they were doing to try and save him. It was going to get colder out here after dark, especially in this rain, and he probably wouldn't last long if they didn't get him home.

Lisa knew that April and Samantha would have heard all the shooting too and must be worried; wondering what in the heck was going on. If Mitch and the others were back they would surely come to investigate, but they couldn't count on that. She and Stacy both gave Uncle Benny a quick hug and she looked at Tommy one last time before she turned and took off, wiping the tears from her face as she ran.

* * *

The boy running back to tell the others had not gone far when he heard more shooting from behind him. The first shot sounded like his father's rifle, but then there was something else, and then the rifle again. He hesitated but knew better than to disobey his father's order. Thankfully, he didn't have to go a half-mile before he ran into six of the other hunters. They were on foot and already coming down the road to investigate, having heard the gunfire.

"We heard shooting," the first to speak said.

"Yes, we found a herd of cows. My dad got two of them and hit another one. He said to come back and tell Mr. Drake and the rest of y'all to get on down there with the horses. He said tell him to send somebody back to tell the others too. He said there would be a feast tonight and that we'd round up the rest of the herd tomorrow. There was some more shooting after I was already running to get you, but I don't know what that was about."

"Did you see anybody around there where those cows were?"

"No, but my dad says there must be a house nearby. That's why he wanted me to hurry back and get everybody. He says we're going to have a new place to stay and plenty for everybody to eat for a long time!"

Before the man could reply, even more gunfire echoed

through the woods from the direction from which the boy had come. But this was a popping crack rather than the thunder of a deer rifle. And it was round after round, going off in evenly spaced, one-second intervals.

"What the hell?"

"That sounds like a .22. That's not Kenneth or his boy, Kenny. We'd better get down there and see what's going on!"

The man who'd been questioning the kid turned to him with another order. Jimmy, we're going to slip on down this road and see what's going on. Your old man and your brother might need some help. You run on back the way we came and get Mr. Drake. You'll find him and the others waiting with the horses. They're back there around the last couple bends to the west. Now get!"

Eight

WHEN APRIL HEARD ANOTHER rifle shot some fifteen or twenty minutes after she had gone back inside, she knew something unusual was going on. Benny and the girls had still not returned to the house, despite the increasing rain; and neither had Tommy and David, who should have had time to finish making their rounds by now. It would be dark in another hour, and everyone but Mitch and the guys would be back before then. Maybe they would too, but she knew it depended on the outcome of their hunting.

She barely had time to get to the door to look outside again when she heard another gunshot, a booming one that sounded like a shotgun instead of a rifle. *Was that Benny?* When two more rifle shots followed the shotgun blast, April stepped outside on the porch, almost running into Samantha, who was trying to rush inside to get her.

"Something is going on out there, Samantha!"

"I know. This is really weird. Why would they be shooting so much?"

April didn't have time to answer before another sound

from the same direction reached their ears—the rhythmic firing of round after round from a smaller caliber weapon. It went on and on, each shot almost exactly the same amount of time apart from the last. April didn't count them, because she hadn't expected the shooting to continue like that, but when it finally stopped, she and Samantha were staring at each other.

"That sounded like a semi-automatic .22. I wonder if it was Lisa?" April said.

"She emptied a whole magazine if it was."

"I know. There's no logical reason I can think of for wasting ammo like that. Benny would never allow it, and Lisa would know better anyway."

"What are we gonna do? Do you want me to go check on them? I know you can't leave Kimberly."

"No. We both should stay here because if you go by yourself you don't know what you'll run into out there. Maybe Tommy and David will be back soon, unless they're out there too. It could have been Tommy's rifle we heard, but there's no way to know. We need to just wait, but I want to stay outside where I can hear. With this rain hitting the roof it's too hard to hear anybody coming shut up inside. Go get your rifle and let's keep watch. If there *is* somebody around that's not supposed to be here, we need to be ready. I'm going to look in on Kimberly and I'll be right back in a second."

Though she'd put on a calm face in front of Samantha, April was filled with dread as her mind raced with the possibilities of what could be happening. The last thing she wanted to think about was more trouble, but she knew that in the reality in which they now lived, it could and probably would come again, and maybe already had. She reached over and stroked her daughter's hair as she slept, careful to keep her touch light so as not to wake her, then shut the bedroom door and went back outside.

"Someone's coming now!" Samantha whispered, nodding in the direction of the gravel lane that connected the house to the road out front.

April heard it too, barely audible in the rain, but unmistakably the sound of running footsteps pounding the crushed rocks of the drive. She stood there with Samantha watching, her carbine in hand, until two figures rounded the bend and entered the yard. It was Lisa and Stacy, and they were running like they were running for their lives.

"Tommy's been shot!" Lisa screamed, when she saw them waiting there on the porch.

"Shot? Who shot him? Where are Benny and David?"

"I don't know, but whoever it was that did it, he was hiding across the road. There was another one too but Uncle Benny shot him! They killed two of my dad's cows and shot Tommy. Tommy might die, April!"

"Is it that bad, Lisa? Where is he? Is Benny with him?"

"It's *real* bad! He got shot in the side, but Uncle Benny said it missed his heart. David is staying there with him until we get back. Uncle Benny went to try and catch the other one that shot Tommy before he gets away. We need help getting Tommy, April! Uncle Benny told us to get the travois they haul the wood on and use it to move him. I was hoping Mitch and them would be back."

"They're not. We haven't seen him. They must have gone farther today. They may not be back tonight at all."

"I wish he was here. Mitch could track down that guy easy. I'm worried about Uncle Benny, and I wish he wasn't going after him alone. But he wouldn't let any of us go with him. He said we had to get Tommy back to the house but we had to be careful moving him or he might die."

April was trying to process all these staggering developments. It was simply unbelievable how quickly everything could change, but she'd had a bad feeling ever since she'd heard those first rifle reports. *Poor Tommy!* He was such a nice and friendly man and he'd already suffered one grievous wound when Wayne Parker had shot him through the arm with a broadhead arrow meant for the center of his back. Now, according to Lisa, he'd been hit in the chest with a high-powered rifle. He might die no matter what they did, from the way she described it. April couldn't imagine what was going through Benny's mind. He would stop at nothing to find the shooter, not only because of what he'd done to Tommy, but to stop him from trying to come back. These trespassers were clearly desperate and brazen to shoot someone's cattle inside of a fence. They had to have known there were people around taking care of them.

Benny had left David there with Tommy until the girls could get help moving him. Now April faced the dilemma of deciding who would go. They couldn't all go because of Kimberly, and she, of all four of them was the most experienced at facing these armed confrontations. What if there were more of them than just the two they knew of? Benny had taken a big chance going out there alone to find out, but April understood why he did it. She wanted so badly to go and help, but Kimberly was her first responsibility and she would have to stay here with her. With everyone else away, it was up to her to make the decisions about what to do. With Samantha's help, Lisa and Stacy could return with the travois. Then with David, there would be four of them to move Tommy back. Maybe by the time they got there, Benny would be finished with his task as well. April knew he was a competent woodsman and that if he had enough time before dark, he would find the other shooter.

* * *

David Green promised Benny he would wait there beside Tommy until the girls returned or he got back, whichever was first. Benny didn't want to leave his boy's side, but he wasn't going to let whoever shot him get away with it either. David would have gone with him, but he understood they couldn't leave Tommy alone. Somebody needed to stay there with him and Benny told David it was best if he did. He had Tommy's rifle to guard him with and he had to make sure Tommy's bandages didn't come loose so he wouldn't bleed too much before they could move him.

Benny said if they could just get him back to the house Tommy would be okay, but David wondered if he was really going to die anyway. Lisa and Stacy had been crying when they saw how bad he was shot and Benny looked really worried too. David kept whispering to him as he sat there beside him, telling him his daddy was going to find whoever did this to him. David didn't understand why anyone would shoot a nice person like Tommy. Tommy never hurt anybody as far as he knew and all he was trying to do was run off that boy that had shot those cows. David wondered now if the person who shot Tommy would have shot him instead if he had been the first one to get there, and he figured they probably would have. That boy was walking towards Tommy while he was hurt and on the ground, and David just knew he was going to cut his friend open the same way he was doing those steers when they found him. That's why he ran out from where Tommy had told him to wait and hide, to try and stop the boy with his spear. When he missed, he could tell the boy was going to try and kill him too, and the only reason he didn't was because Benny shot him with his shotgun.

It was just Tommy's bad luck in the first place that he was the one in front and the first one to step out in the open. Tommy always led the way when they were on patrol together because he knew where they were going and David didn't.

David just followed along wherever he went because Tommy told him to, and he didn't have much of anything else to do anyway. Without Tommy, David wouldn't have known what to most of the time. Tommy said the reason they went out and walked the fences every day was to check and make sure they were okay and that the cattle were still inside them, and also to keep an eye out for strangers. They never saw any before today, but Tommy always carried his rifle in case they did. David didn't have a rifle but he carried the long, sharpened stick that he called his spear and he often glanced back along the path behind them to make sure they weren't followed. Tommy had told him there were bears and panthers in the woods and he told him all kinds of scary stories when they were walking. David believed every one of them because he didn't have any reason to doubt what his friend said. Ever since he'd come here, following Mitch out of the woods, he'd liked Tommy and it wasn't long before he considered him his best friend in the whole world. Now someone had shot him just because he was trying to save the cows. It made David sad to see him looking like he looked now, his jacket and shirt soaked in blood and his face contorted with pain as he lay there trying to breathe.

David was glad Benny had shot the one with the knife, and he hoped he would get the other one too, before it got too dark to find him. Before he left, Benny said the strangers must have come there by way of the road from the west, because that was the way to get here from every place else.

THE FORGE OF DARKNESS

Benny said he was going to head that way, staying in the woods alongside the road, because he said he thought the other one would probably circle back to it and try to go that way to get away. But Benny wouldn't let him get away if he could help it. He was going to make him pay for what he did to Tommy, and David didn't feel sorry for whoever it was at all. *Nobody* had the right to shoot Tommy, and David wished he could shoot whoever did it himself.

Nine

THE SHOOTER ACROSS THE road wasn't sure how many adversaries he was facing. He had seen the man with the rifle approaching his son initially, and had taken him out, but then the other one had charged out of nowhere like a madman, throwing a spear. Then, from the woods in the direction the rest of the cattle had run, another one had slipped up on Kenny and shot him with a shotgun. It was such a pity he didn't see that one in time to save his son, but the visibility was poor in the woods in this rain, and even with the scope he'd not been able to pick him out from where he was hiding. The boy had been ambushed and didn't have a chance. He'd figured all along something like this was going to happen to that one; it was just a matter of time. Kenny was overconfident and far too often, careless. He shouldn't have left his rifle leaning there against a tree out of reach while working with his knife. If he'd been paying attention, he would have heard those two coming and could have shot them on sight and been done with them. But even if he had, there was the other one with the shotgun neither of them had seen.

That was the problem with reacting to and focusing on one threat while assuming it was the only one. His son had paid for his mistake with his life, and now there were even more unknowns. All that .22 rifle fire had come as another surprise. It sounded like someone emptied an entire 25 or 30 round magazine in his general direction, not really knowing exactly where he was. His position behind a solid hardwood stump gave him both cover and concealment, so he just hunkered down until the shooting stopped. It wasn't worth giving away his location to shoot back and he knew they would stop eventually. When they did and he was able to look again, he saw they had dragged the body of the one he'd hit to where they were hiding. It didn't really matter, because after a hit like that he would die soon if he wasn't already dead. Kenny was lying where he'd fallen, his rifle still propped against the tree where he'd left it.

Nothing moved as he watched and waited to see what they would do next. Would they go back to wherever they came from with the wounded or dead one he'd shot? Or would they try and get across the road and outflank him? He figured that probably depended on how many of them there were. Little Jimmy had gone to get the others and it wouldn't take them long to get here, so he figured his best bet was to sit tight unless he saw something that made him think otherwise. As soon as it was clear, he would cross the road to where Kenny had fallen, but after studying him through the riflescope, he didn't have to get any closer to know his oldest son was already dead.

* * *

Leaving his boy lying there bleeding and in pain was the hardest thing Benny Evans had done since he buried his wife in their backyard over eight months ago. But Tommy was either going to survive this or he wouldn't. It didn't matter whether all of them were there or not, because there wasn't much they could do for him until they moved him to the house. But Benny knew he was the only one among them who could go after that shooter and catch him, and he aimed to do jus that. It was far too dangerous for David or the girls and he knew that even with his experience he had to be careful or he would get himself shot too.

They never saw any movement across the road and still didn't know exactly where the rifleman was hiding, other than somewhere on the wooded hillside. The sniper had the advantage of the high ground and concealment, but now that the light was fading Benny knew it would be harder for him to pick out a target. As long as he stayed well within the trees on his side of the road, Benny figured it would be safe to try and circle around on him, crossing the road somewhere farther down, in the direction from which he was sure the strangers had come.

Benny knew it was possible the shooter had already

slipped away. It was doubtful that he would stick around and make an attempt to retrieve any of the stolen beef after coming under so much fire, and especially losing his partner too. The dead one was just a teen-aged boy, probably not much older than Lisa and Stacy. Benny wondered if the one who'd shot Tommy might be just a kid too, but it didn't matter. Whoever it was had aimed to kill his boy and Benny was going to make sure he didn't get away with it. It was going to be dark soon and Benny knew he had to hurry or finding him would be impossible.

He crossed the fence when he came to the boundary of the Henley property and pushed on through the adjoining national forest lands that bordered the road on both sides there. Benny figured he needed to parallel the road for a few hundred yards and then find a place to cross it, unless he happened to see the shooter before then. The woods beyond the farm property consisted of plantation pines set out by the forest service just a few years prior. They had not yet been thinned, so the thickly growing trees provided good cover, but because of the dense branches, he had to stay quite close to the road to keep within sight of it. He figured if the shooter were trying to get away, he would take to the road again as soon as he left the area of the confrontation.

When Benny had gone far enough to be well beyond the first bend in the road from the place where the shooting had happened, he slipped up the edge of the gravel to look and listen. It was empty as far as he could see in either direction.

To the west, where it led off to the outside world, it curved away out of sight within a quarter mile. When he heard nothing and saw no movement either on the road or in the woods on the other side, Benny stepped out of the trees and quickly made his way across. The gravel here was hard-packed, so unfortunately there would be no footprints, even if not for the rain washing them away as soon as they were made. There was no way to know if his quarry had already made it to the road and was even now beyond the bend, or if was still somewhere between here and the place from which he'd shot Tommy. But Benny was betting on the latter of the two possibilities, because he figured anyone concealed as carefully as he had been would also be careful about moving out. He would have to have been practically running to get beyond this point otherwise. If he was wrong, Benny knew he might get away for good, but he made his choice and decided he would carefully work his way back in that direction, slipping through the woods on that side of the road until he hopefully intercepted him. In the dim light and falling rain, he figured that when they did meet, it would be well inside of shotgun range.

Benny was about to start moving that way when he happened to glance back down the road to the west one more time. What he saw at the point where the curve began stopped him in his tracks. Six shadowy figures, spaced well apart and moving slowly like they were expecting an encounter, were advancing along the road in his direction. All of were them carrying long guns at the ready, like they expected to use them any minute. Benny couldn't make out the details of their faces since all were either wearing hats or had hoods of their jackets pulled over their heads because of the rain. The six men were eerily silent as they advanced, using hand signals to maintain stealth as they moved.

It was clear to Benny that they were coming to investigate the source of the recent gunfire, but this was completely and utterly unexpected. He had to assume these strangers were with the other two, and if that were true, the one he sought might not try to escape after all. Instead, his friends had come to help, and now Benny was faced with a far bigger problem than he'd imagined. Six armed men were more than he could take on alone with his shotgun and he needed to somehow warn the others of the danger. But now he was on the wrong side of the road and couldn't cross again until these men passed. And by the time they were safely out of sight from where he stood frozen now, they would be closing in on David, waiting alone and unsuspecting there with Tommy. Benny's head was exploding with all these developments. Seeing his boy shot like that and knowing he would be lucky to survive it was already enough to deal with for one day. Now everyone else he cared about was in jeopardy too. If there was ever a day when he wished Mitch was not away hunting, this was it.

Benny had only been standing a few yards from the edge of the road when he'd first seen the approaching six. As he processed what was happening, he barely had time to slowly sink to his belly in the low-growing ferns around him before they were near enough to see him. He watched with his finger on the trigger of the shotgun as they slowly slunk by, scanning not only the road ahead but also the ditches and surrounding woods. Benny was afraid to even blink and he was certain that if it hadn't been raining and wasn't nearly dark, they would have spotted him lying there.

He was way too close to them for comfort; certainly close enough to get a good look at what he was dealing with. All six were grown men, unlike the teenager he'd shot. They were heavily bearded to a man, all of them wild-eyed and looking like they had been living outdoors for months, as was to be expected these days. One of them carried a shotgun—a pump like Benny's but with an extended magazine like the riot guns the police sometimes used. The rest were armed with military-style semiautomatics: AR-15s and AK-47 variants. They were moving in silence, communicating with hand signals like they were in a war zone expecting enemy contact at any minute, and Benny knew if he was spotted he was a dead man. But after several excruciating minutes during which he barely dared to breathe, they passed by his position. Benny remained motionless as he watched them go, until the one bringing up the rear was at least a hundred feet down the road. Stepping as carefully as he'd ever done in his life, Benny eased his way back to the road and quickly slipped across again. He had to follow these men, but he wanted to be on the same side of the road as Tommy. The girls would not have time to get back with the travois before these men got there and David had no idea they were coming. It looked grim for all of them, and Benny didn't see a way out of what he knew was surely coming.

Ten

TIME DIDN'T USUALLY MEAN much to David Green because he had no memory of anything beyond the recent past and little concern for any future beyond the present day. The only life he knew revolved around the Henley farm and most days since he got there had been the same until this one, when everything suddenly changed. But sitting there waiting with his helpless friend, it seemed to David that the minutes were dragging by impossibly slow. He wanted the girls to hurry up and return with April or Samantha and the travois they were going to use to get Tommy home, and he wanted Benny to hurry back too. But it seemed like he'd been waiting there forever. It was still raining and the dim light was turning to twilight. David and Tommy were alone except for the dead boy Benny had shot and the two steers the strangers had killed. David didn't want to be out there waiting when it got dark, but he didn't think Benny would come back until he caught the other one that shot his boy. He kept whispering to Tommy, telling him he needed to try and get up on his own if he could. He said the others might not come back for him and that it would be dark soon. He also told Tommy he was sorry for what happened to him.

"You didn't deserve to get shot, Tommy. All you were doing was what you were supposed to—protecting the cows. They shouldn't have shot you for that, but they did. I wish I could have stopped them from doing it, Tommy. I really do, but neither one of us knew there was another one hiding over there across the road."

Tommy's eyes were open and he seemed to hear him but he didn't respond. David could see that he was still breathing, but he was too weak or in too much pain or both to talk. Benny had slowed the worst of the bleeding by packing the entrance and exit wounds with strips of cloth ripped from a flannel shirt he'd been wearing under his jacket. The crude bandages were soaked through with blood, but they were effective in blocking most of the flow. Benny had warned David and Lisa that when they moved him onto the travois they would have to take care that the bandages did not come loose.

David thought he heard something in the woods behind him and he looked anxiously in the direction Lisa and Stacy had gone to get back to the house. He hoped it was the two of them coming back, but he waited and waited and there was nothing. Then he looked back to the road and saw something move over on the other side. His heart pounded in his chest as he watched for it again, and then there it was: a man stepping slowly out of the woods and into the open by the edge of the road. Even in the poor light, he could tell by the man's shape that it wasn't Benny. He was much too tall and thin, for one thing, and he moved differently. David reached for Tommy's rifle with shaking hands and twisted to get a better view through the trees behind which the two of them were hidden.

The man stood there for what seemed a long time, waiting and listening no doubt, before he walked into the road. David's hands were shaking and he was having a terrible time trying to control them. He knew this man had to be the one that shot Tommy, and probably the steers too. Now he had emerged from hiding and was coming to see about his friend that Benny had shot. He probably thought they were all gone because it had been a while since the shooting stopped and nothing moved after Benny and the girls left. But David knew that once he got over here by the dead one, he would look around and he would find them. He had to stop him while he didn't suspect anything and before he had a chance to shoot first. David steadied the rifle by resting the forearm stock against the side of a tree. That helped stop the shaking and he was able to line up the open sights on the man's chest. David didn't remember where he'd first learned to shoot, but it somehow felt familiar to him every time he did it and it came natural enough that he knew he wouldn't miss at this range. He was just about to pull the trigger when he heard a voice that caused the man in the road to turn and face the other way.

THE FORGE OF DARKNESS

David hesitated and turned his attention to the direction the man was now staring. It was the same way Benny had gone and he wondered if it could be him, but the man called back to whoever it was in a friendly tone. Then David saw that there were several other men walking down the road. They were carrying guns and they seemed to know the one who'd shot Tommy. David didn't know what to do now. If he fired the rifle at the one he was aiming at, these others would know he was there and he didn't know how many of them there were. Even if he didn't shoot he was afraid they'd quickly find him and Tommy if he just waited there. The first man was already pointing to his dead companion as he spoke to the others, no doubt telling them what happened. And the body was less than twenty yards from where he and Tommy were concealed. David knew he was about to run out of time if he didn't do something fast.

* * *

"We're not going to find him before night," Mitch said, turning to face Jason and Corey, who were following close behind him. "It's too dark to follow the trail. We need to find a place to camp and look for him at first light."

"There won't even *be* a trail in the morning," Jason said. "All this rain will wash what little blood there was away."

"It doesn't matter. He's probably already lying up somewhere and may have already bled out. We'll find him in the morning."

"We should have just gone back to the house then," Corey said, "got a good night's sleep and started out fresh. It's going to suck, camping here out in this."

Mitch knew Jason and Corey would gripe about spending the night out here in the rain. He would have preferred to be back at home too, especially now that April was there. But part of his reason for deciding to stay out was for the benefit of his two apprentices. They needed to appreciate the consequences of a less-than-perfect shot, and the difficulties of tracking wounded game in tough conditions. The more uncomfortable they were, the better. It was no big deal to Mitch, because he had been doing stuff like this for fun since he was old enough to follow his dad. He still loved it now, even though it meant a night away from April. It was great having her there, but with all the others now living there too, the house sometimes felt crowded and confining to Mitch. He would always need his time away in the woods, through preferably in better conditions than this.

But Mitch had come prepared for a night out in bad weather, as he usually did on hunts like this. In the small backpack he wore there was an eight by twelve ripstop tarp, the grommets already fitted with lengths of paracord to secure the corners. He selected a spot near the creek on a slight rise where the rainwater would drain and stretched another piece of heavier line between two trees. With this to serve as a central ridge, it was a simple matter to rig the tarp into a makeshift A-frame. They were already wet from trailing the deer in the rain, but at least they wouldn't have to sleep out in it all night.

"Well, I guess this is a good opportunity for you guys to practice your wet weather fire-building skills."

"Great," Jason said. "Then we can sit around it and eat cold venison jerky. Sounds like a party to me!"

"Well, it could be worse. At least we have the tarp... and the jerky..."

"It could be better, too," Corey said. "We could all be back at the house, eating a real supper and sitting by the fireplace. It's going to get cold tonight. Wouldn't you rather be spending it with April than the two of us?"

"Nah, I can do that any time. This will make her miss me and it'll be better than ever when I get back tomorrow!"

"Well, if it was me in your shoes," Jason said, "I wouldn't give a girl like her the *opportunity* to miss me. I wouldn't let her out of my sight! The only bad thing for you I guess is that she comes as a package deal. How's it feel being a dad at freakin' 17, dude? And what are you going to do if David ever gets his memory back? You see that kind of thing with amnesia in movies and stuff. Somebody gets hit in the head, loses their memory for a while, then it all comes back to them all of a sudden. Boy, when it does, I reckon he's gonna be pissed, seeing you've taken up with his girl and his kid and all!"

"Yeah, he's gonna realize the kid's really his. He thinks

she's just confused about that right now and he's going along with it because he thinks he should."

"I'm not worried about David. April told me it had been over between them for a long time, probably three or four months now. They broke up way before she talked him into helping her sneak out of Hattiesburg and come out here. Even back when I helped her get there, things weren't that good between them."

"Yeah, but that doesn't mean he won't be jealous. He's bound to be. You said he was the first time you met him. He's not going to like it when he realizes he's been replaced."

"Yeah, but it won't matter. It's not up to him anyway. It's April's choice. Besides, we don't *know* that he'll ever get his memory back."

"He's sure as shit doesn't know anything right now; he's almost like a little kid. The way he follows Tommy around you'd think they were a couple of ten-year-old school buddies."

"Yeah, Tommy's kind of simple, but he's solid. I always feel pretty good when I'm away, knowing Tommy and Benny have got the house. They're good people, and Benny's a real woodsman. Both of them are. They'd have to be, living out of a canoe for nearly seven months the way they did. And you guys are bitching about one night camped out in the rain… You've already forgotten how good you've got it!"

Mitch knew they had not really forgotten; he was just giving them a hard time, trying to make light of their discomfort. Jason had been beaten nearly to death in the early days after the collapse, and Corey had found his parents murdered and his family home ransacked and burned. Both of them were survivors, and they were doing fine considering their total lack of experience at this kind of thing in their lives from before. Mitch was sure they would find Jason's deer nearby in the morning, and soon after, the three of them would be packing meat back to the house, another successful hunt completed. As he imagined April's arms around him again, he also thought back to the three gunshots they'd heard that afternoon. Tomorrow he would find out what that was about as well, although he was sure it wasn't anything significant.

Eleven

LISA AND STACY RAN to the barn to get the travois and found it still piled high with firewood that Tommy and David had left on it that morning. The two of them quickly tossed the load of cut logs aside and then practically ran back to the house pulling the empty rig behind them. It was a great design Benny had come up with shortly after he and Tommy arrived there with April. Seeing how far they were having to go into the woods to carry wood, he looked around the barn and found a wheel from an old mountain bike Mitch had broken in half years ago jumping ditches. Benny had mounted it between two long support rails made of oak lumber he also found in the barn, carving handles at the towing end so that it resembled a stretched wheelbarrow one person could pull behind while walking. The travois was narrow enough to weave through the woods yet stout enough to haul two or three hundred pounds. The loading surface was narrow but wide enough for Tommy to fit as long as they were careful not to dump him off on a bump. Lisa figured if David could do the towing, she and Samantha could walk alongside him on either side and make sure he stayed aboard.

Samantha was ready to go when they reached the house and was carrying her rifle and a couple of blankets to put under and on top of Tommy. April watched from the porch, Kimberly in her arms and her carbine slung from her shoulder: "Be careful!" she warned. "Don't fool around out there; just get Tommy and get right back as quickly as you can. If Uncle Benny doesn't find whoever shot him, Mitch will when he gets back in the morning!"

They hurried down the drive at almost a jog; the fastest pace Stacy could pull the travois. Samantha was behind her with her rifle and Lisa was in front, taking point with her 10/22 carbine, for which she now had three extra magazines in her pockets. Lisa knew that April really wanted to go and would have gladly taken her place in the lead, but Kimberly had to come first for her, so she would wait this one out. Lisa was determined to make that wait as short as possible. When they were half way to the road, she turned off into the woods to take the shortest route back to Tommy. They had just entered the trees when she heard the sound of someone running, crashing through the underbrush and apparently coming right at them. Lisa stopped and motioned to Stacy and Samantha to do the same. She barely had time to raise her rifle to her shoulder before a surprised figure burst into view, almost on top of them. Lisa's finger had just found the trigger when she realized who it was.

* * *

Benny was moving slow and stealthy through the woods, careful to stay back, well out of sight of the six men he followed. They were far too alert and too much on edge to risk shadowing them close, and besides there was still the other shooter to think about. Benny still had no idea where he was, so he had to consider the possibility of being spotted by him with every move he made.

As he pushed his way quietly through the wet pine branches, he wondered what David would do when he saw these other strangers. The men were bound to find the two dead steers, because they were plainly visible from the road. Then they'd spot the body of the dead boy he'd shot, lying just a short distance from where David and Tommy were hiding. When they closed in to investigate the scene, would David be able to keep his composure and remain quiet? Or would he panic and start firing at them at once? Benny didn't know what to expect from David. *Hell, the boy didn't even know who he was!* What he did know though, was that if he started shooting at those six men, he might get lucky and get one or two, but the rest would kill him quickly. Then they would find Tommy and it would be over for him too.

Benny was trying to come up with a plan, even as he eased closer. Six armed men in a group and another unaccounted for didn't make for good odds in an outright gunfight. Then, there was the issue of the girls coming back with that travois for Tommy. They had no way of knowing these other men had arrived and Benny had no way to tell them, unless he circled around and tried to get to the house or meet them before they got back so he could head them off. But that would leave Tommy and David vulnerable. It was a choice Benny had to make, but Tommy was his *boy*. He had to see what was going on. Maybe... just maybe... if David could keep his composure and remain quiet... the strangers wouldn't discover the two of them immediately. Then he might have a chance of somehow diverting their attention, drawing them away. He considered doing that even now, firing into the air or something to lure them back the other way, but the problem with that was that there were enough of them that they might split up. Then, some of them would still find Tommy and he wouldn't be able to help, being occupied with evading those who were looking for him. At any rate, it was probably already too late for that. They'd had time to reach the spot of the shooting already, and Benny was half expecting at any moment to hear David fire Tommy's rifle and then all hell to break loose. But that didn't happen. Instead, what he heard was something else, a sound completely and totally unexpected, coming down the road behind him from the west, just as the six men had.

Benny turned at this new sound, peering through the branches to see. He had no doubt about what he was hearing; the sound was unmistakable. His eyes proved him right when the first of the horses appeared around the bend. Benny counted eight riders and at least as many more saddled animals on a string behind the one bringing up the rear. The horses were approaching at a trot when he'd first heard the sound of their hooves, now the lead rider raised his hand and the riders slowed their mounts to a quiet walk. Benny was absolutely stunned. *Where in the hell had all these men come from and what was he going to do now?* He'd thought it couldn't get any worse when he saw that the cattle rustlers had six more companions. But now it was clear that there were more than twice as many yet again! This explained why the first two had been brazen enough to shoot into Doug Henley's herd inside a fence on private property. There were enough of them that they felt they could do what they wanted with complete impunity.

Twelve

DAVID WORKED QUICKLY TO pile leaves over Tommy as quietly as he could. He didn't know what else to do. He had to retreat farther into the shadows before the men were on top of him. There was no possibility of moving Tommy by himself. To drag him, he would have to stand up and they would immediately see him even if they didn't hear all the noise that would make. All he could hope for is that they wouldn't look too closely and wouldn't spot Tommy lying there under the leaves in the darkening woods. When he had done the best he could, he crawled backwards, working his way into some low-growing bushes another ten yards away. The men were crowded around the dead one now and he could hear everything they said:

"I'm sorry they got Ken Jr., Kenneth. Did you see how many of them there were?"

"I saw three in all, but I think there was at least one more. First, there was the one that slipped up along that fence line and got the drop on Kenny. He was saying something to him, probably about the cattle, and he was pointing a rifle at him. I decided I'd better take him out before it went too far. I hit him dead center and he went down, but then this other one comes running out of the woods all crazy-like and throws a spear at Kenny! It missed him and Kenny moved in on the lunatic with his blade. I was gonna let him have at it, because I could see that the fool didn't have a weapon, other than that stick spear he'd already thrown. Kenny would have gutted him easily, but then I hear a shotgun blast from out of nowhere and see Kenny go down hard. He never had a chance because some other son of a bitch neither one of us knew was there ambushed him! I tried to shoot the one that had been carrying the spear, but he dove into cover with his buddy somewhere behind those trees over there. Then somebody else opened up on me with what sounded like a . 22. I'll bet they must have shot 20 rounds!"

"I know; we heard it."

"When the shooting finally stopped and I looked up, they had moved the one I knocked down. I guess they dragged him back to wherever they came from. I never saw any of them again after that. I waited a while to make sure, and was finally coming down here to see about Kenny when I saw y'all coming."

From what he'd heard already, David gathered that the man who had spoken was the father of the dead boy Benny had killed. He was bent down over the body now, and David could hear what he was saying:

"Kenny, I don't know what you expect me to tell your

mama now! I've been telling you over and over again you needed to be more careful. I thought you'd listen eventually, but you never did, and now it's too late. I hate it for you, son. I really do. All I can tell you is that we'll find those folks that shot you and they'll pay. We'll kill them all and round up every last one of their cattle. There's a house around here somewhere and we'll find it. If any of them are still in it, there won't a one of them be alive come daylight. I promise you that, Kenny."

"How many head was in that cattle herd?" David heard one of the others ask the man as he got to his feet again.

"I counted 25, including those two over there. I hit another one but didn't put it down."

"Well, if that's the case there'll be enough to feed everyone for weeks, just on the beef. And there'll probably be other stuff in the house when we find it. I'd say we scored pretty good on this one, Kenneth, other than losing your boy."

"I've been expecting it to happen. But there's nothing any of us can do about it now. How far back is Drake with the horses?"

"He's close. We sent Jimmy on to get him. They should be here any minute. But you know the others probably won't get here for a couple of days. The rain ain't helping; you know how it is."

"It doesn't matter. When Drake shows up there'll be enough of us to do what needs doing without them. We don't need to wait for them. We can go ahead and find the house and get moved in."

"Yep, and if the folks that shot at you were dragging a wounded man, there ought to be a trail," one of the other men said.

"Let's find it then, before it gets too dark," another said.

David's worst fear came true in the next instant. All of the men were walking straight towards the clump of trees where Tommy was lying hidden under the leaves! David didn't see how he could stop them from finding his friend now. There were too many of them for him to shoot them all by himself and Tommy was helpless, unable to move. All David could do was watch as the men began combing the ground looking for sign.

"Well would you look at this!" one of them said with delight. "Hey Kenneth, it looks like your new friends gave up on their man and lit out for home! They tried to bury him before they left, though!"

"Is he dead?" One of the others asked as he walked up to the one who'd found him.

Before he answered and before David could grasp what was about to happen, much less react, the man who he now knew was the dead boy's father stepped up as he reached for something behind his back. Then he suddenly knelt down and hit Tommy hard with it, the sound of the impact a dull whack that made David shudder when he heard it.

"I don't really think he was, but I *know* he is now, the

sorry bastard! That was for Kenny, and I'll get the one that shot him too!"

When the man stood back up, David could now see that he was holding what looked like a hatchet or tomahawk in one hand. *He had just hit Tommy in the face with it—hit him and killed him right in front of his eyes and there was not a thing he could do about it!* David wanted to shoot them all. He wanted to make them pay for what they did to his friend, but if they killed him too, who was going to warn Lisa and Stacy? And what about Samantha and April with her little girl back at the house? This was turning out far worse than Benny had thought when he left to look for the one who'd shot Tommy. There were so many of these men! And they were talking about even more people that were further behind, all of them coming here too! David knew he had to get away alive. He had to warn the rest of his friends what was coming. It was too late to help Tommy but maybe he could save the others. He didn't know where Benny was or if he was even coming back and there was no time to look for him. Besides, these men could have already found him and killed him too. David just didn't know.

He remained as still and quiet as he possibly could until the men lost interest in Tommy and turned to discussing their plans for finding the house. As soon as they moved farther away to regroup by the road, David wormed his way backwards on his belly until he felt it was safe to stand. Then he turned and ran back towards the house for all he was worth, practically running right into Lisa, who was aiming her rifle at his face when emerged from the woods into her view.

* * *

"David!" Lisa whispered as she lowered her rifle. "What are you doing? Why are you running? We've got the travois to get Tommy."

"It's too late, Lisa. They killed Tommy! One of those men killed him!"

Lisa could see that David was both terrified and overcome with sadness. "What do you mean they killed him? Are you sure he's dead? Did he die from the gunshot?"

"No. It wasn't the gunshot, Lisa. But it was the same man that shot him. It was that dead boy's daddy. But there are a *lot* more of them too, Lisa! That's why I couldn't help Tommy. I wanted to, but there were too many!"

"You mean there are more than we thought? Where is Uncle Benny now?"

"Yes, a lot more. They came from down the road the way Benny said he thought the other two did. I don't know where Benny went. He went in the woods and didn't come back. The men that came after that all have guns, Lisa. And I heard them talking about even more of their friends coming that are on horses! They were talking about finding our house and killing everybody in it and eating all the cows!"

"You heard them say all that? Samantha asked."

"Yes! I heard everything they said. I was hiding really close. I tried to cover Tommy up with leaves and hide him too, but they found him anyway. And then that man that shot him hit him right in the face with a hatchet!"

"Oh my God! You saw him do that?"

"We were too late," Lisa said, before David could answer. "This wouldn't have happened if we had gotten here sooner and moved Tommy before they found him."

"We came as fast as we could though," Stacy said. "How could we know there were more men coming?"

"We couldn't have," Samantha said, before turning back to David: "I'm so sorry, David. I know Tommy was your best friend, but you did the right thing. There would have been no point in you dying too, trying to save him."

"I didn't know what to do," David said.

"Samantha's right," Lisa said. "But are you sure they didn't see you, David?"

"No. They didn't. I waited until they walked back over by the road before I moved. I knew you were coming and I wanted to stop you before you got there. Those men will kill you if you go there, Lisa. They killed Tommy like they just didn't care! If Benny had been there to help, we might have stopped them, but I don't know where he is and he might be dead too!"

Lisa said she didn't think so, but she wondered how far away Uncle Benny could be to not see or hear so many men coming down the road like that. The only explanation she could think of was that he was well away from the road, off in the woods trying to track down the one that shot Tommy in the first place. When he didn't find him, would he return to where David was supposed to be waiting with Tommy, unaware these other men were there and run right into them? It was possible, but then she remembered that Uncle Benny was a real woodsman, like her dad and her brother. Surely he would be careful. It wouldn't do any good for the four of them to go looking for him now with all those strangers already intent on finding the house. And April was alone there with Kimberly, unaware of the much more serious danger they were now facing.

"We've got to get back to the house," she said. "There's nothing we can do for Tommy, and we don't know where Uncle Benny is. We've got to tell April what's going on and we've got to do it before those men get there first. Just leave the travois here. We don't need it now. Let's go!"

* * *

April had been pacing the living room floor with Kimberly since the moment Samantha and the girls disappeared down the drive. She couldn't help but worry with them going out there while the trespasser who'd shot Tommy was still unaccounted for. They didn't know that he wasn't still lurking around and there was no guarantee Benny would find him. Of all the nights that Mitch could pick to stay out hunting, this had to be the worst. Since she'd arrived there, he'd only done this one other time, when he and Jason and Corey had been unsuccessful until the third day of a hunt. Mitch had told her then when they returned that he expected their hunting would be taking them farther afield, as the deer were becoming too wary closer to home. Providing for eleven people was putting a lot of pressure on the local game.

She'd felt safe enough with Benny and Tommy around, especially since they'd started regular patrols around the property, but now Tommy had been shot. From the way Lisa and Stacy described it; it was bad, too. Lisa told her Benny said the bullet passed all the way through, and that it missed his heart, but it was impossible to know what it *did* hit and how much damage had been done. She just hoped they could hurry and get him back here and that Benny would get back too. She would feel a lot better when they were all inside the house, then they would see what they could do for Tommy. She had cleared off the big, sturdy wooden table in the dining room and moved the chairs out of the way. The first thing they needed to do was get him onto that where they could see what they were doing. She'd helped Mitch patch up Jason in that very room when he'd been nearly beaten to death, but he didn't have a bullet wound through his chest. Surviving that would be iffy even with the attention of ER doctors in a fully equipped hospital. April tried not to think about what it would do to Benny if he didn't make it. He'd already lost his wife and Tommy was all he had until the two of them found her and then Mitch took them in as part of the family.

She walked to the door and went out on the porch again to stare down the road. She knew the girls probably had not had time to even reach the spot were Tommy and David were, much less get back with him, but she couldn't stop herself from watching for them anyway. When they suddenly appeared, running fast to the house with someone else with them, April thought she was seeing things. But they were real indeed when they drew closer, and she could see that David was the forth person running with them. *But where was the travois? And where was Tommy?*

Thirteen

"WHAT DO YOU MEAN, Tommy's dead?" April asked as Lisa blurted it out even before the four of them reached the porch.

"David saw it. Those men killed him, and they're coming here next, April!"

It took her a minute to get them all to slow down and stop talking at once. April was trying to keep Kimberly calm, as she was getting upset by all the commotion and had begun crying. Lisa and David were saying that a whole group of armed men were now out there by the road and that David had heard them talking of finding the house that they knew must be nearby.

"They said they were going to come here and stay. They were talking about all the cows and how there would be enough to feed everyone for weeks when they all got here."

"How many of them do you think there are, David?"

"I don't know. There were six of them that came down the road after the one that shot Tommy came out of the woods. But I heard them talking about some people coming with horses... and then they said something about a bunch of women and children too."

"It's like there's a whole mob of them!" Lisa said. "What are we going to do, April?"

April's mind was racing with this overload of bad news. Tommy was dead and now they were facing a group of killers intent on taking everything they had. Who were these people and where did they come from? Were there really as many of them as David thought? She hoped not, but in truth, she had no reason to doubt him. Since he'd been hit in the head he saw things in the simplest ways and it would not even occur to him to embellish his story for effect. He'd just witnessed his new best friend killed with a hatchet and he was both scared and angry, but he was also concerned about the rest of them, who he considered his friends too. They were the only people in his world now, and he liked them all. April had to take his warning seriously, and from what he said, they had very little time to prepare.

If Mitch and the rest of the guys were here, they would handle this differently. But with three of them off hunting, Tommy dead, and Benny unaccounted for, they were five men short for any kind of serious resistance. Mitch and Benny had often discussed ideas for fortifying the house for just such an event, but they had not had time to get very far with it; the daily patrols being the main thing implemented since April arrived there. After the encounter with the four men who'd abducted her and Kimberly, Mitch knew they were vulnerable to desperate survivors who might be on the move looking for resources. But he acknowledged that they couldn't prepare for everything and the most important defense was to remain vigilant, until they could become more organized. Finding enough food took up a large portion of Mitch's time, not to mention the efforts of teaching the others the essential skills they needed, such as marksmanship, archery, tracking and hunting.

Mitch would be sick to find out the thing he'd feared would happen had come to pass while he was away for the night. But that was something he would have to deal with tomorrow. April had to make a decision and she knew she had to make it quick. If there were as many men as David said and indeed more on the way, there was no way they could defend the house from an attack if it came before Mitch returned. And after all the shooting that had already happened, April was sure that these men wouldn't wait. They knew there were people living nearby and that they probably had resources they wanted. They would come tonight, she was sure of it.

"We can't stay here," she told Lisa. "We've got to grab as many of the things we need as we can carry and get out of the house now!"

"But we can't let them break into our house!" Lisa said. "This is all we have! How will we live without the house and all the stuff we need?"

"We're not going to let them have it, Lisa. Mitch will be

back tomorrow. You know that. But if we lock ourselves inside and try to defend it with just the five of us they may take it anyway, after they kill us all. You know that kind of thing has been happening ever since the lights went out. If we're trapped in here and surrounded, we won't have a chance if there are enough of them. I don't think we should risk it, Lisa. We can hide close by in the edge of the woods and wait and see. Maybe they won't come here tonight, but if they do, at least we'll have options. The guys will be back in the morning and Benny is out there somewhere too. They will come up with a plan then, but if we don't go now, it may be too late."

"I know you're probably right. It just feels like giving up or something. It's sucks that we've got to leave our house and sit out in the woods in the rain all night."

"Believe me, I hate to have to take Kimberly out in this weather too, but better that than risking her life in a gunfight. We don't know what those men might do. These walls won't stop rifle bullets."

"I just hope they don't find us out in the woods anyway after they find out we're not in the house," Samantha said. "It would be even harder to fight back out there."

"They won't find us." David said. "I know all the good places to hide. Tommy showed me."

"And, we can go all the way to the creek if we have too," April said. "The canoes are hidden there if we need them. The important thing is that by getting out we will have options. But if everybody is in agreement, we need to hurry! We need to think fast and get everything we can carry that we might need."

"All the guns!" Lisa said. "We've got to take the guns and ammo, or they'll steal it all if they break in.

"Within reason," April said. "What we can't carry we can lock in the safe. We have to take food too… and blankets and tarps for shelter… we need matches, something to cook in… knives… extra clothes…" April's mind was racing even faster than before. There was so much to consider, but of course it would be impossible to take everything they might need. Of course they couldn't carry all the firearms, much less the ammo that was stashed away. She didn't want to loose anything to theft, but she had to hope for the best, that these people would either change their minds and leave or Mitch and Benny would come up with a way to thwart their plans before they got far.

Kimberly was her first priority and she knew she could not personally carry much else besides her child and the essentials she needed to take care of her. She was nearly two now and could eat what the rest of them ate, which was crucial because there was little left of the well-stocked larder Mitch's parents kept in the house as a matter of course before the pulse. Hunting and gathering had become essential for survival and back during the summer, before April arrived there, Mitch and his sister and friends had done what gardening they could with seeds his dad had left from the year before. But now they were into early December and though the winters were mild here, it was still more difficult living off the land than it was in the warmer months of the growing season.

Lisa was right. It *did* suck to have to leave the warm, dry house and hide out in the rain because of the threat of violence from a gang of ruthless trespassers. April had hoped there wouldn't be more of this kind of life-or-death drama for a while, but here it was, visiting again so soon after her last ordeal of terror. There was no time to dwell on that though. The five of them quickly ransacked the pantry, gun safe and closets and moved their supplies out on the front porch to sort things out and figure out how they were going to carry it all.

"I wish we hadn't left that travois behind now," Lisa said.

"We weren't thinking about having to do something like this," Samantha said.

"No, I was just thinking about getting back to warn April."

"It's okay," April said. "We don't know that we'll have to go far. Let's just get everything we can carry across the yard to the edge of the woods. Then we can make another trip if we have time."

April hoped they *would* have more time than they needed. Maybe because of the weather, the trespassers would camp out there by the road where they'd shot the cattle and sit tight until morning. If they did, that would give her and the others more options and would mean less time to wait on Mitch to return. She was holding out on this hope after they stashed the blankets and some of the guns in the woods and were heading back to the house for a second trip. They were halfway across the yard when they heard a strange sound coming from out in the direction of the road. It was a horn of some kind; a primitive sound like something from a medieval battlefield in a movie. It came as one long, eerie wail and ended abruptly, the echo drowned by the falling rain.

"What was *that?*" Stacy wondered.

"I'll bet is a signal. They are using it to let the rest of their friends know to come on!" Lisa said.

"Yes, I think you're probably right," April said. "That means we don't have much time. We've got to hurry and grab the other stuff and get out of here!"

"You should stay back and wait with Kimberly, April. There's no point in taking her back to the house because you can't carry much with her anyway. We'll get the rest of the stuff."

"Okay, but just hurry! They may be coming this way right now!"

April stood there watching, trying to soothe Kimberly as she waited at the edge of the yard for the four of them to gather up the remaining gear and supplies on the porch. They made it back to where she waited and after moving everything into the edge of the woods; they stood listening for that strange horn again as the rain continued to fall softly around them.

"Hey…do you hear that?" David asked.

They all stopped whispering and listened closely. It wasn't the horn, but something more subtle. At first, April didn't recognize the sound as she had really only heard it when watching television or movies in her prior life in the city. But Lisa recognized immediately what it was and when she named it, April knew she was absolutely right and David had heard the men mention them too: *horses! It was the sound of hooves clattering on the gravel, and it sounded like there were a lot of them.*

"I hear voices too!" Stacy whispered.

"Yes, it sounds like they're out by the end of the lane," Lisa said. "The gate is locked, so that may slow them down, but they'll probably break it down or cut the fence to go around it."

"I think you're right," April said. "They're getting ready to come to the house and nothing is going to stop them. We'd better get this stuff farther into the woods and make sure they don't see us when they do."

Fourteen

MUCH TO HIS DISMAY, Benny found himself virtually trapped between the six men he'd been following and this other band of eight who'd arrived on horseback. The problem was that the riders decided to stop in the middle of the road almost adjacent to where he was hiding when he first spotted them. They had inexplicably picked this spot to sit tight, apparently to wait for a signal from the others. Benny cursed under his breath as he watched them dismount. Two of them walked to his side of the road and relieved themselves at the edge of the bushes less than 20 feet from where he stood. Once again, Benny was almost afraid to breathe as he watched and waited. He could not extricate himself from this situation to get back to Tommy for fear of being discovered by these riders, who were clearly following the other six who had gone ahead on foot.

As he stood there watching, Benny studied the men and their equipment, trying to figure out where they might have come from. He and Tommy had been living deep in the woods along Black Creek for most of the time since the

THE FORGE OF DARKNESS

blackout, so Benny had not had much contact with the outside world and what was going on there. Mitch and the others had told him what they'd seen of it, and April especially, had seen more than her share during the time she was sheltered in the church in Hattiesburg. From what they said, Benny gathered that many places were virtual war zones now, with large gangs fighting for control of territory and the goods necessary for survival. The grid had been down for nearly nine months, so Benny figured there had been enough time for this violence to evolve from random looting and crimes of opportunity to something much more sinister. What he saw before him certainly looked like the latter. These men seemed organized, well prepared and experienced in what they were doing. They were far from a random gang of thugs from what he could see, and Benny figured they'd probably been raiding and pillaging all the way from wherever they'd come from, whether nearby in the region or from much farther away. Whoever they were, they appeared to have adapted well to the harsh conditions of life as it was now. They were well at ease with their horses so Benny figured most of them already had plenty of time in the saddle before the blackout. But how did so many come together and agree to a mutual plan? Surely they had a leader they believed in to cooperate that way. Benny didn't know the answers, but he knew their arrival was bad news for the Henley farm. Life as they'd known it up until today was about to change forever once again.

It had already changed for him with Tommy getting shot. Benny didn't know if anyone could survive a wound like that without medical care, and now it probably wouldn't even matter. Even if the girls got him back to the house, how would they hold off a gang like this until Mitch returned? And even if Mitch *was* there it might not matter. Benny knew as he stood there watching that they had made some serious mistakes. They had talked about it, but they had not managed to implement more serious security measures. It wasn't that they didn't all agree on the need, it was simply that it was hard to secure and defend 600 remote acres with road access on one side and a navigable creek at the back. The patrols were enough to deter random trespassing, and if the cattle rustlers today had indeed been two wanderers as Benny had first thought, that would be one thing. But this was something else all together.

The men with the horses were taking great precautions, holding back to wait on the other six, but of course they didn't know they were being watched. The twilight was fading to full dark as he waited, and Benny was growing more anxious by the minute. He kept hoping the men would mount up again and move on, but they didn't, and he again began to think how he could extricate himself from his position without being detected. He might have a chance to help Tommy if only he could get to him, but the longer he was trapped here the more likely that chance would evaporate. Benny began his escape with a single step away from the road, but was stopped mid-stride by a sudden, unexpected sound. It was someone blowing a cow horn, and it was coming from the east along the road where David and Tommy were, and where the six men on foot had to be by now. Benny didn't know if it meant they had just found the dead steers and boy, or perhaps David and Tommy as well, but it was clearly the signal the men with the horses were waiting for. He saw the riders mount up and move on, closing to rendezvous with their friends, as he turned and disappeared into the woods.

* * *

"I'm sorry about your son, Kenneth," Drake said as he dismounted and walked up to the other men to get the story.

"Yeah, me too, Drake. He messed up, but I just want to get ahold of that son of a bitch that shot him."

"Do you know where the house is yet?"

"Yeah, that's why we gave you the signal. Mosley and Hanberry did some recon. There's a gravel driveway that turns left off of this road about a quarter mile east of here. It leads straight to a house, and there's a barn too. They didn't get too close, but that's bound to be it. It's the only turn off on this road anywhere around here, and it's gated at the entrance and inside this same fence where the cattle are"

"We don't really know how many might be living there though, do we?"

"No. We found the one I shot and I put him out of his misery, but there's at least one more, probably two, that were with him. Kenny Jr. was killed by a shotgun loaded with buckshot, but I was also under fire from what I'm pretty sure was a semi-auto .22 rifle."

"That may be all they have but you never know. We need to be careful. I don't want to lose anybody else."

"I agree. I think we ought to move in and hit the house tonight before they can get prepared if there are more of them. This nasty weather is on our side and hitting them now won't give them time to regroup or go for help."

"That works for me. We'll secure the house immediately and have it ready when everyone else gets here tomorrow. If there's anyone to put up a fight we'll take them out and be done with it tonight. If they run off, they probably won't be back once they figure out we're not just a handful of vagrants. This is a good find, Kenneth. It's remote enough to give us some security, and the cattle are a nice bonus. Let's hope there are more goods around the farm as well."

"Farm girls would be nice," one of the other men said.

"Now you're dreaming, Chuck. I think the only females you're likely to find out here are in that herd of cattle."

"Don't be so sure about that. Besides, a man can dream, can't he?"

"How do you want to do this, Drake?" Kenneth asked.

"Let's split up into three groups. We need maybe four guys on foot to go on ahead through the woods on both sides of that driveway, in case anybody's hiding out there or tries to run out of the house. Let's get them moving now. We also need a couple guys to stay here with the extra horses and keep an eye out in case they come back looking for their dead buddy. The rest of us will hang out here at the road and wait for the signal that all's clear at the house, or else move in with everything we've got if there's resistance. We'll ride down to that gate right now and cut the fence for the horses. But once we're done at the house, we need to fix it quick. We don't want to lose any of that herd."

"That sounds like a plan," Kenneth said. "But I want to be the first one in that house. I want a shot at that bastard that killed Kenny if he's home or shows his face. I'll give you a quick three rounds from my pistol once we're done to let you know everything's clear."

"You bet, Kenneth. Pick who you want to take with you and get going! The sooner we get this done, the sooner we'll be carving up steaks and sleeping indoors again, out of the rain!"

Drake had a good feeling about this place. Most of the land for miles around was uninhabited national forest and houses and farms were few and far between. Anyone living out here before the grid collapsed would have lots of the necessities for self-sufficiency already. Finding a place with cattle still fenced in was a windfall for sure, and Drake was willing to bet there would be other things of use at the house and barn. He wouldn't be surprised to find running vehicles, or at least a tractor, as well as fuel, tools and firearms and ammunition. It would be nice if the house was a big one, but even if it wasn't, he was sure that with the barn it would accommodate the rest of his little tribe. He hoped the remoteness of the place would mean they could stay awhile. They were all tired of moving, especially the women and children, and he'd lost too many good men in confrontations along the way. It would be good to regroup, let the wounded heal, and make a new plan for a long-term strategy. Drake considered that setting up here; in a place like this could *be* their long-term strategy. He knew that Black Creek was nearby, running roughly parallel to the road they were on and winding through the woods somewhere in the back of this farm. It might be the perfect place to call home, but first they had to rid it of any occupying vermin. It would be best if they *did* resist, so he and his men could quickly kill them all. If they simply ran away, they might come back later with help or may tell others who would come to challenge them in the future. Drake liked doing things right the first time, and in his recent experience, killing most people outside of his little band who got in the way *was* the right way. He paced his horse back and forth on the road near the entrance to the long lane after cutting a gap next to the gate with the wire cutters he carried in one of his saddlebags. He and the other men were anxious to get moving, and hoping for a brief taste of battle before settling in for a big feast later that night.

Fifteen

ONCE THEY'D MOVED THEIR gear deeper within the cover of the woods, April asked Stacy and Samantha to stay there and keep Kimberly quiet and out of the wet, wrapped in a poncho she'd grabbed on the way out. She wanted Kimberly far enough from the house for extra safety while she and Lisa and David crept back to the edge of the yard to watch and see what was going to happen next. She felt they were relatively safe even so close, because after hearing the sound of horses she was sure these thugs would be riding down the driveway when they came. For some reason though, they still had not come any closer, and it was not until Lisa whispered that April knew why.

"I saw somebody move over there in the woods on the other side of the yard!"

April stared where she was pointing and at first saw nothing, but then there *was* a movement. Two figures stepped out of the shadows and quickly crossed the yard to the other side of the house, momentarily disappearing from her view. If it were just one person, she might have thought it was

Benny trying to get back inside undetected, but two working together meant that they had to be with the cattle rustlers.

"It's a good thing we're not in the house," David whispered.

"Yes, they're checking it out to see if anyone's home."

"We could shoot them when they show themselves again," Lisa said.

"Not now. We don't know how many there are out at the road, and all that would do is bring them looking for us. Right now they don't know if there's anyone around or not. Maybe they won't look too hard tonight if they think whoever lives here has left."

"Look!" Lisa whispered again.

April saw the two men come around from the back of the house to the edge of the porch. Seeing them there, pressed up against the wall a hundred yards away, she had to admit it was tempting to shoot them both dead right now. They had killed poor Tommy and it made her sick to think about it. And she knew what was coming next. They would ransack the only place she and her friends had left to call home, taking everything of use unless Mitch and the guys got here in time to stop them.

She watched with a sinking feeling as the two men stepped up onto the porch and crossed to either side of the door. After what seemed like several minutes but was probably less than one in reality, she heard a crash as one of them kicked the door in and then saw them go inside. April was about to whisper her disgust to Lisa and David when she heard a branch break with a dull snap clearly audible even in the rain. The sound was close—somewhere nearby among the very trees in which they were hiding—somewhere between them and the end of the driveway! *Whoever had stepped on that branch was sneaking through the woods on the same side of the yard as they were!*

That Lisa and David heard it too was confirmed when April glanced at them and saw them staring back at her wide-eyed and speechless. She didn't know if Stacy and Samantha could have heard it from where they were; she just hoped they stayed quiet. The sound was subtle and it was only one pop, but she had little doubt that it was a person. It took something heavy to snap a branch like that. And seeing how those other two men had crept up through the woods from the opposite side of the yard, it made sense that there might be one or two more sneaking up from this side. If so, then they knew what they were doing and were not taking foolish chances. Whoever was in the woods here was probably waiting to see if the two going inside would flush anyone out of the house. Even though she'd been tempted, April was really glad now she'd made the decision not to reveal their presence by firing at those first two. She didn't dare move now. Would the unseen stalkers step out into the yard now and walk over to the house after their companions? Or would they continue moving inside the wood line and walk practically right into her and Lisa and David? She expected to

119

hear another footstep that would give her a clue, but what she heard instead was far worse: *Kimberly!* Her child suddenly cried out from deeper in the woods, no doubt catching Stacy and Samantha by surprise before they could react in time to hush her. When they did quiet her just a second or two later, April was sure it was already too late. Whoever was in these woods with them had to have heard it as well as she. She focused on the direction from which the breaking branch sound had come and crouched there ready to shoot as soon as a target presented itself. But the next sound she heard was not the subtle sound of a stealthy footstep, but instead more gunfire, coming from out by the road. It sounded like a shotgun; two blasts in quick succession! *Could it be Benny?* After those two shots she heard the sound of running horses again as well, but April could not let herself be distracted long by that distant commotion. She had to keep her focus close at hand, because she was certain someone was there in the woods with them—someone who would not go away without investigating the cry her frightened child had made.

* * *

Benny had worked his way in close and now he could hear the voices of several men talking where the horsemen had joined the other six. He was close to the place where the steers and the teenaged boy lay dead, and where he'd left David and Tommy hidden behind the cluster of trees. Benny had circle around, and was approaching from the back, as far from the road as possible. He still didn't know if first six that had gotten there had discovered David and Tommy, or if their signal just meant they'd found the dead boy and animals. Benny figured he would have heard David fire Tommy's .308 if he'd been discovered, but he didn't rule out the possibility that he'd lost his nerve and ran.

It had gotten dark enough that he could hear some of what the men were talking about before he could see them. They were splitting up, and he heard several of them ride down the road in the direction of the driveway on horseback. After waiting and listening for a few more minutes, he was sure all of them were gone except for two that were waiting there with some of the extra horses.

Benny crawled through the undergrowth until he was within mere feet of the trees behind which he and David had dragged Tommy after he'd been hit. He couldn't see anything in the dark to indicate David was there, but there was a shape sprawled on the ground that he knew was his boy. Benny whispered softly, calling David's name in case he was hidden nearby, but there was no response. He could just make out the two men standing over by the horses on the edge of the road, but nothing else moved that he could see. So David *had* left!

Disgusted at the thought of a coward who would abandon his friend to save his own skin, Benny slowly crawled the rest of the short distance to where Tommy lay, whispering his name as he took his boy's hand. When he drew himself closer, to look at Tommy's face to check that he was still breathing, Benny recoiled in horror at what little he could make out in the faint light. Touching him to confirm that what he was seeing was real, Benny knew immediately that Tommy was gone. His boy's face was a ruined mess of blood and shattered bone. Benny felt his whole body wracked with rage and sorrow as he knelt there for a moment over Tommy, the tears rolling across his cheeks and into his beard. Then, not caring if he was heard or not, he rose to his feet and walked directly to the men standing there with the horses. Sensing his presence or perhaps catching a glimpse of movement, the two of them turned his way, startled by the sudden appearance of a shadowy apparition with long white hair and beard stepping out of the darkness. Whatever thoughts of surprise may have entered their heads at that moment were the last thoughts either of them ever had. Benny made sure of that with two rounds fired from hip at point blank range.

The sudden blasts from the 12-gauge sent the horses standing nearby into a panic. As they dashed away down the road to the west, Benny grabbed the rifles the two men had dropped and melted back into the woods. As much as he wanted to wait there to kill as many of the other men as he could to avenge his boy, he had to think about those two teen-aged girls who called him their uncle, as well as Samantha and April with her child back at the house. The only one he didn't care about was David, who'd run off and let his boy be murdered. But Benny should have known he couldn't count on a fellow like that who'd been hit upside the head so hard he didn't even know who he was. And now he knew he should have never gone off and left Tommy there to begin with. He'd foolishly thought he was dealing with just a couple of hungry desperadoes but he'd been terribly wrong and Tommy had paid for his misjudgment with his life. Benny didn't want to live with himself after that, and if it were just him he would have surely made his stand right then and there, fighting to the death. But even as this thought crossed his mind one more time, the sound of gunfire erupted from the direction of the house and Benny took off, certain he was the only hope those girls had tonight.

Sixteen

APRIL'S HEART NEARLY STOPPED when she heard a man's whisper from just yards away in the dark woods. Her suspicions someone else was out there besides the two already in the house were proven true in an instant and now she knew there were at least two more of them. And from the conversation that ensued, she knew they had heard Kimberly's cry as clearly as she and Lisa and David. But like the three of them, the unseen stalker was startled by the two shots from out at the road. That was obvious by what he said to whoever was with him:

"I wonder what in the hell that was about?"

"Maybe Drake and them found the one that shot Little Kenny."

"Maybe, but whoever did it would have to be dumb to hang around out there in the same spot. I figured he would be around the house by now. We ought to go see what Kenneth and Chuck found inside."

"What about what we heard before?"

"It was probably nothing but a cat or something. In fact,

I'll bet that's what it was."

"It sure sounded more human-like to me. It sounded like a little kid crying."

"We're on edge though, you know that. If it's like most farms, I'll bet there are a few cats hanging around that barn. If there was anybody living in the house that had a little kid, I'd wager they'd still be holed up in there, trying to hide. Either that or they're long gone already, hiding off in the woods somewhere. The one that shot Kenny or the one with that .22 could have run back here to warn them, if there was anybody here to warn. Come on. We ought to go see what they found in there. Whatever the shooting was about out there, Drake can handle it and you can bet he'll be riding up here any minute with the rest of them. We got here first, so we ought to get first pick if there's anything special inside. If we wait, we're going to miss out. In fact, we might be missing out now. Maybe Kenneth and Chuck *did* find someone hiding in there. Maybe they found a girl like Chuck was saying."

"Maybe. I'll tell you what. You go on ahead and I'll be right along in a minute. I'm just going to take a quick look over there first."

"Suit yourself, but I doubt you'll see that cat in the dark."

April felt the adrenalin flood her body, as she now knew that what she'd feared was inevitable. Out of the corner of her eye she saw the man who'd dismissed the sound step into the edge of the open yard. Her focus though, was on the shadows in the direction from which their voices had come.

Her Ruger Mini 14 was at her shoulder as she waited for a form to materialize from out of the gloom. When it did, the man had to be less than 10 feet away from the muzzle of her rifle. April couldn't make out the details of his face, but when she was certain her sights were centered on it, she squeezed the trigger. The man dropped like a stone and she quickly turned her attention to the other one that was in the yard. She needn't have worried about him though. Before she could get him in her sights, she heard the crack of Lisa's .22 rifle and saw him fall too, likely shot in the head as well.

"Good shot, Lisa! Now let's go!" April wanted nothing more than to grab Kimberly and get as far away from here as possible. David didn't hesitate to go with her, but Lisa did. April heard her open up with the .22 again, firing several rounds at the front door of the house as one of the men emerged. It looked like he was hit, but in the next instant bullets were shredding the trees and branches around them as the other one opened fire on them from inside with an automatic weapon.

"LET'S GO LISA! WE'VE GOT TO GET OUT OF HERE NOW!"

Lisa listened to her this time and the three of them quickly reached Stacy and Samantha, April taking Kimberly into her arms as she slung her carbine over her shoulder and prepared to run.

"Is anyone hit?" she asked, feeling for Lisa and David in the dark.

"I'm not," David said.

"Me either. But I wish we'd gotten that other one! He's got a freaking machine gun!"

"Mitch will take care of him later, Lisa. We've got to get out of here now. Those other men with the horses will be swarming the house any minute. There's nothing else we can do here. We've got to get to the canoes and find someplace safe to wait!"

Lisa didn't argue further. They'd gotten two confirmed kills and maybe a third, but none of them had any illusions about being able to drive off all the intruders if there were as many as David said. They needed to put some distance between themselves and the house before the rest of those men began combing the woods looking for them. They left most of the supplies they'd brought from the house right where they'd put them on the ground. There was no time to be burdened with loads that would slow them down.

April let Lisa lead the way through the dark woods because she knew the lay of the land better than anyone other than her brother and dad. With the creek not far away and several canoes hidden nearby, at least they had options. She just hoped they could warn Mitch and the other guys before they returned. April was disgusted at the thought of filthy strangers ransacking Mitch and Lisa's family home. She was sure they would take everything of use or value in the current environment, and they might destroy the rest out of pure meanness. They'd already killed some of the cattle and

David had heard them talking of rounding up the entire herd. But the most atrocious thing they could do was what they'd done to poor Tommy. Tommy was such a sweetheart and a good, innocent man. He, of all people did not deserve such a fate. Nor did Benny deserve the heartache of losing his only son. And April knew he might well be dead too. There was simply no way they were going to know tonight. All she could hope was that tomorrow revealed some answers and some ideas for a course of action. She couldn't imagine what their lives would be like if they couldn't rid the house and property of these trespassers. The Henley farm represented the center of their universe now. The house provided shelter and in it and the barn were the tools and other things they needed to survive in a world where getting more goods from the outside was out of the question.

* * *

Mitch was restless after nightfall, feeling confined and bored in the minimal shelter of the tarp. It would be uncomfortable even alone, but it was miserably crowded to share it with two other guys. There was little they could do to pass the time while stuck under it in the rain. Jason and Corey were keeping a small fire going near one end, but that was mainly because Mitch had insisted they build it to practice their wet weather fire building technique. It wasn't really cold, but the light was welcome and the flicker of the flames at least gave them something to stare at as they sat there talking.

Dinner had consisted of strips of venison jerky they were each carrying with them, and didn't require cooking anyway. Mitch dreamed of roasting the backstrap of Jason's fresh kill over the fire instead, but that wasn't going to happen tonight. The jerky was dinner and would be breakfast in the morning too. Mitch didn't mind, but he couldn't help thinking how nice it would be back home out of the rain, in the house with April. What made those thoughts better was that he knew she would want that too.

Mitch had been infatuated with April from the beginning, especially after seeing how she handled herself in that first violent confrontation when he'd met her. He soon discovered she was a city girl completely out of her element in the woods, but that was okay. At least she was willing to learn and she'd done just fine, even in those first few days. Mitch had never met anyone who fascinated and captivated him the way April did, but he'd been careful not delude himself with wishful thinking. After all, she was nearly two years older and she already had a child—a child who had a father. Her only goal in life at that time was to get back to her daughter and Mitch had assumed after he helped her do so and said good-bye that would be it.

He knew she'd been impressed with his archery skills and his knowledge of woodcraft, but that was understandable considering the situation they found themselves thrown into. In normal life, she wouldn't have even noticed him and he'd figured even if she did, she wouldn't have been interested in him, even if she had no one. After all, he was just a high-school country boy from rural Mississippi who had little knowledge of the kind of lifestyle she'd lived before the collapse. That she'd actually come back here looking for him seemed like a minor miracle. And not only that, she came not just because she needed refuge for herself and her child; she came because she wanted to be with him again.

When Mitch had found David lost and filthy and disoriented in the woods, he didn't even know April and Kimberly had been rescued from the man who had taken them. He had been shocked to see her at the house, and he'd assumed she would be thrilled he brought her fiancé (or husband by now, for all he knew) back alive. She was glad to see David had survived after being left for dead, but Mitch soon found out the feelings she'd once had for him had long since cooled to bare tolerance of his presence. He *was* Kimberly's father, but that's all he was to April, and as it turned out, it was convenient for both April and Mitch that David no longer remembered his prior relationship with her.

They had talked a lot over the days that followed, and he had been delighted just to be in close proximity to her again. Of course it wasn't the same as those first days he'd known her, when it was just the two of them traveling together; facing dangers that increased by the day in a world that was coming apart around them. It was different now, with nine other people living in the same house with them, so they had

131

far less time alone with each other, but still, there was some. Mitch began giving her serious instruction in shooting the bow and arrow, and in return, she was teaching him some basic movements from her father's martial art that she'd put to use so effectively more than once since the blackout. It was one day while doing this when they were in close contact, she showing him how to break free of a chokehold, that she suddenly put her arms around his neck and pulled his face close to hers and kissed him full on the lips. Mitch had been taken completely off guard by that move; which proved far harder to defend against than the attack scenarios they'd been training. But he wasn't complaining. Her kisses were more wonderful than he'd imagined in the frequent daydreams he'd entertained since they met. It had been all too brief, that magical first moment in her embrace, but she'd promised there'd be more, *much* more to come.

She'd told him nothing would ever come between them again after that day; but Mitch was still the most skilled and productive hunter among their small group. And it was his job to show the others and make sure they acquired the skills they needed, too. And so here he was, crowded under a tarp with two guys in the rain. Mitch tightened the drawstring of his jacket hood to snug it around his face, and curled up on the ground between Jason and Corey. When he closed his eyes he hoped sleep would come quickly and erase the hours until daylight. Then he could find that deer and go home to her again.

Seventeen

DRAKE WAS WAITING FOR the signal from Kenneth and the others who'd gone to scope out the house. What he hadn't expected was more shooting back at the spot where Kenneth's son had been killed. Two reports, one right after the other from what he was sure was a shotgun, followed by the sound of horses taking off in panic was not good. There had been no return fire or other sound from Marcus or Bobby, who were waiting there with the extra horses and watching the site. Whoever killed Kenny had used a shotgun, so Drake figured the odds were pretty good that the same person had come back for more.

It took stones to pull off something like that with so many of his men nearby, so to Drake it was obvious they were dealing with a dangerous adversary, or at least someone unafraid to die. Either way, the elusive shotgunner could not be dismissed as some clueless farmer. It wouldn't do any good to go charging down there on horseback only to get more of his men shot, so Drake whispered to the others gathered around him and four of them dismounted and entered the woods on foot. Two of them would work their

THE FORGE OF DARKNESS

way back through the trees alongside the road to where
Marcus and Bobby were supposed to be waiting and the other
two would cut through the woods between there and the
house and try and slip up on the crafty shotgunner from
behind. Drake had no intention of wasting time chasing
down the horses that had run off. They would either come
back on their own or instinctively run back west the way
they'd come from until they eventually met the rest of their
people bringing up the rear.

The signal he had been waiting for from the house never
came. Right after the four men he picked moved out to look
for the gunman, Drake heard two rifle shots, the second one
unmistakably a .22 rimfire. Then, a couple seconds later, there
were more rounds from the .22, and then several 3-round
bursts back-to-back from an M4.

"That's got to be Chuck!"

"Yep! It sounds like he and Kenneth have run into
trouble. Let's go!" Drake urged his mount forward, taking the
lead down the driveway. He didn't want to run into an
ambush, but the shooting stopped after the staccato bursts,
so he figured Chuck and Kenneth might already have the
situation under control. The shotgunner was still out there
somewhere, but Drake was confident his other men would
eliminate that threat shortly. Once he and the rest joined up
with Kenneth at the house, there would be enough of them
to set up defenses to make sure no one could return if
anyone who'd lived there was still hiding out nearby. In a

couple more days, all of his people would be here and he intended to make it safe for them beforehand. As he rode down the driveway, even with the possibility of a gunfight at the other end, Drake couldn't help but take in what little he could see of the property in the dark and the rain. He would know more after having a good look around in the morning, but so far he could already tell he liked what he saw.

* * *

The darkness closed around her, reminding April of her first nighttime trek there with Mitch when she had known nothing of the woods. She had trusted that he did though and had agreed to follow him and help him in exchange for all he was doing for her. It was a dangerous mission, going out at night to rescue Lisa and Stacy from the depraved Wallace brothers who had taken them, but it was something Mitch had to do. April remembered her terror at every unfamiliar sound as the two of them walked through the dark woods and paddled down the inky black waters of the creek. Her fear of the wild was a natural reaction for someone who had lived her entire life in cities, and Mitch understood. But each life or death situation she'd encountered had proven him right; the real threat was from her fellow humans, not the wild creatures inhabiting the forest.

Now that April understood this, she had no hesitation about fleeing into the forest, even on a gloomy wet night such as this when it was difficult to even see where to place her next step. When she stumbled over something unseen on the ground and almost fell, David offered to carry Kimberly for her and April let him. Kimberly, of course, had no objections to going to her daddy, even though poor David didn't really believe he was. But at least he was willing to play along with it, despite his memory loss, and for that April was grateful. She knew it was a bit selfish of her to think this way, but David was so much more useful and agreeable to be around now than he was before he got smashed in the head by a rifle butt. For his sake, she hoped he regained his memory, but she didn't look forward to having to deal with the "old" David if and when he did.

April wished they could find Mitch and Jason and Corey tonight, but Lisa had assured her that wouldn't be feasible and that it would be a waste of effort to try. April knew she was right even before she suggested it. The guys wouldn't have stayed out at all if they were still close to the house, not to mention they would have heard all the shooting if they were anywhere nearby. In the tens of thousands of acres of national forest lands that bordered both sides of Black Creek, finding them at night, or even in the daytime for that matter, would be practically impossible. The best she could hope for was that they could intercept them in the morning, before the three of them returned to the farm and unwittingly ran into the intruders now occupying it. It terrified her to think of that happening, because they could all be shot before they realized what was going on if they simply walked into the backyard unaware.

April had voiced this concern to Lisa and she agreed. Lisa was certain that Mitch and the others had gone downstream, as that was the way to his favorite hunting grounds. She said if they took two of the canoes and paddled down to the next bend, they could camp on the sandbar that was across the creek there. They would be out of reach of the killers if they came looking for them, but close enough to Mitch's return route that he would probably spot them on his way home. April dreaded what would come next once Mitch learned what had happened in his absence. Her worries for him would be just beginning at that point. He would be outraged at the idea of strangers in his house and on his land, killing his father's cattle. And if that were not enough to make him declare war, learning of Tommy's murder would send him over the edge of fury.

She was afraid for him because she knew there was no other choice he *could* make than to stop at nothing to drive out these men. This was not a fight he or any of the rest of them could simply walk away from. The house and barn and the tools and other things in them were all they had. They were going to have to take their farm back, not simply for revenge but as a necessity for survival. April couldn't help but dread the thought. Just as she'd allowed herself to feel somewhat safe again, her world had once more been upended in a matter of hours. Would there ever be a respite from this uncertainty? Lately, she had dared to hope there might be, but now she doubted it. Her father was fond of saying that change was the only thing that *was* real in the world, and that any semblance of stability or permanence was in fact an illusion. Back then, his stories of the old Zen masters and their teachings that he passed along as part of her instruction in the martial arts were hard for her to grasp. But over time, especially after she lost him, she began to understand that he was right. It wasn't long after his death that she lost her mother as well, and then, like everyone else she knew, she lost *all* the comforts of the world in which she had grown up. In the blink of an eye it had fallen apart; the effortless communication and connectivity, the artificial insulation from heat, cold and rain, and the rest of the manmade safety nets that created the illusion of separation from nature.

April had adapted quite well to life with that illusion stripped away though. She had accepted change as her father had told her she must if she were to ever understand, and in many ways she found the transition easier than she would have imagined. She had learned new skills and survived challenges she wouldn't have dreamed of in that life before, but still she was weary of the fear and uncertainty; especially the fear of yet more loss. She could *not* lose Mitch. He was the most amazing young man she'd ever met in her life, and she was determined to spend as much of it as she had left with him, no matter how hard or how short that remainder might be. Reaching the creek tonight and finding a place to hide until morning was the first step, if she were to ever see him again.

Thanks to her lifelong familiarity with the land, Lisa managed to lead them unerringly to the bay thicket where the canoes were hidden, despite the darkness. They removed the branches and debris covering two of them and turned them upright to carry them to the water. Mitch always kept paddles lashed to the thwarts in all the boats, so once they reached the creek bank, all they had to do was untie them and go.

Eighteen

"Did you see how many of them there were?" Drake asked when Chuck stepped off the porch to meet him as they rode into the yard.

"No, I couldn't see a damned thing! Kenneth and I heard two gunshots over there at the edge of the woods. One was a high-powered rifle and the other one was a .22 like the one we heard earlier. Hanberry is down, and I'm pretty sure he's dead." Chuck pointed to a body sprawled in the grass at the edge of the shadows. "I don't know about Mosley. I haven't seen him at all, so it doesn't look good. When we heard those shots, Kenneth stepped out the door to see what was going on, and took three rounds from that .22 and went down. I wasn't close enough to the door to see the muzzle flash, so I still don't know exactly where they were shooting from, but I dumped over half a mag into the tree line there behind Hanberry. There wasn't any return fire and they didn't shoot at any of you when you rode up, so I think they must have run off. I still haven't seen or heard from Mosley."

"How bad is Kenneth hit?"

THE FORGE OF DARKNESS

"It's bad, Drake; two rounds through the gut and lower chest, and one in the pelvis; probably hi-velocity .22 hollow points. He's not gonna make it."

"Dammit! And Marcus and Bobby might be dead too! I sent Clint and three of the others with him to try and find that bastard with the shotgun. He's still out there somewhere."

"Yeah, we heard the shots out that way before this happened here at the house."

Drake turned to his remaining men and ordered them to check the area beyond Hanberry's body before asking Chuck what he and Kenneth had found in the house.

"We could tell there were several people living here; some of them women or girls for sure. One of them has a little kid too. It looks like they've been here a long time, probably ever since the lights went out. We were going to check the barn when Mosley and Hanberry got here, but that never happened. There's a game warden's pickup parked out back of the house for some reason."

"Is that right? That could explain the asshole with the shotgun then. Whoever he is, he's got some woodcraft. We'll check all that stuff out later. Let me take a look at Kenneth."

Drake found Kenneth doubled up on the floor, soaked in blood and obviously in a lot of pain. Chuck was right. His chances weren't good. The damned thing about those little . 22 bullets was that they could zip around inside a body once they penetrated, ricocheting off bone in all kinds of crazy directions. There was just no telling what kind of internal damage the three rounds had done. As he sat there lying to Kenneth that he was going to be fine, the other men came back with their report after checking the perimeter:

"Mosley and Hanberry are both stone dead! We found Mosley just inside the woods, shot right between the eyes, and it looks like Hanberry took a bullet in the back of the head. Whoever it was that shot them took off in a hurry though. They had moved some blankets and other stuff out of the house, but they left it piled up and ran, it looks like."

"They probably moved that stuff out there when they first heard the shooting out at the road," Drake said. "Chuck's M4 must have convinced them they didn't need it as bad as they thought they did. I doubt they'll go far in the dark in this weather. Clint and the others will find the one with the shotgun—he's probably in charge here—and we'll track down the rest in the morning. I'm not going to let them get away with killing Mosley and Hanberry, not to mention Kenneth. Chuck's right, he won't last until morning. That's three good men right there, and that's not counting Marcus and Bobby, who I'm afraid might be shot too. And then there was that no account boy of Kenneth's they got first. That's four lost in one raid and more likely, *six!* Damn! It's been a long time since we've had a day like this!"

* * *

THE FORGE OF DARKNESS

Benny moved as quickly as he could in the dark, cutting through the woods on the shortest route back to the house. It was essentially the same route he and Lisa and Stacy had taken that afternoon when they set out to find a Christmas tree. He knew the men on horseback would be using the gravel lane to get to the house, and he wished now they'd done more to make it less appealing to visitors. The lane made it obvious that a house was nearby, even though Mitch had removed the mailbox months before. If the condition of the barbed wire fences and the presence of the cattle weren't evidence enough, in the daylight the house and barn were visible through the trees from certain angles along the road. And while the gate at the entrance might discourage honest passerby, Benny knew men such as these could simply ride their horses around it after cutting the fence.

The extra weapons he carried slowed him a bit, but Benny expected he would need them soon. Both of the rifles he took off the men he killed were imported eastern European AK-47s, modified to semi-auto for the civilian market. Such weapons had been plentiful and cheap at gun shows and pawn shops before the blackout and were a common choice now among the thugs who were out to raid and pillage in the aftermath of the collapse. Benny didn't like them for his personal use, because in his opinion most weren't accurate enough to be worth a damn for hunting. But they *were* reliable and would give him a lot of firepower, even if he only had the single 30-round magazine that was in each when he picked them up.

Benny didn't know exactly what he was going up against, but he knew he needed more than his shotgun. He was pretty sure the automatic fire he'd heard from the house wasn't from an AK though. The rate was different, more like multiple 3-round bursts back-to-back than straight full-auto, and he figured if these men were wasting ammo on spray and pray this long after the collapse, it was probably a common caliber like 5.56mm they could have easily gotten more of in their pillaging. They may have even stolen the weapon from a law enforcement vehicle or taken it from an officer they killed along the way.

Benny hadn't gone far before he came upon the wheeled travois, abandoned and lying over on its side in the leaves. Seeing the outline of it there in the dark was heartbreaking; his hopes it would be of use in getting Tommy safely to the house completely shattered. The girls had not gotten there with it in time, but Benny knew it wasn't their fault. He had made the mistaken assumption that there was only one shooter at large and had left Tommy to go find him. He would have *dragged* Tommy all the way home right by himself if he'd had any idea so many more were closing in on the farm. But he hadn't known, and neither had the girls.

The girls might still be unaware Tommy was dead for all he knew. Since they'd left the travois here, he thought they might have heard the men's voices or the sounds of the horses and turned back to go and warn April. The other possibility was that the men had seen them first and taken them. But the fact that he'd heard a .22 during all the shooting from the house gave him hope the latter wasn't the case. If Lisa was involved in the shootout, she had made it back to the house, but there had been only silence after the burst of automatic fire he'd heard in answer to the .22. Benny didn't want to assume the worst, but there were a lot of bad possibilities. One thing was certain now though—some of the intruders were already at the house. He just hoped April had gotten the warning and gotten her child out in time.

As he neared the yard, he slowed his pace while slipping through the last trees separating the woods from what had once been a well-trimmed front lawn. He'd just heard some of the horses coming down the lane, and as he picked his way to a point where he could see the house from the shadows, he saw several men dismount in front of the porch. Another stranger already inside stepped out of the house to greet them, and Benny figured they were discussing what had happened there with all the shooting. He saw two of the men head for the woods off to one side of the house and that's when he noticed something lying in the grass at the edge of the yard. Benny could tell it was a body, but from where he stood he could not discern if it was male or female, friend or foe.

He still had no idea if April and Kimberly or any of the other girls were inside or not. Because of this, an outright attack on the men gathered there was out of the question, even aside from the great risk it would involve, going up against so many armed men alone. It was a real dilemma for Benny, because if they *were* inside he had no doubt as to what these men would do to them and there wasn't much time to act if he were to get them out. But if Lisa had managed to warn April and all of them had escaped to the woods, it would be foolish for him to hang around near the house and risk getting shot. The only way he was going to know was to get closer, and Benny figured the best thing he could do was to work his way to the side yard where he could see that body. Once he knew whether or not it was one of his friends, he would then study the house and barn from that closer position where he might see or hear a clue as to whether or not any of them were still in there.

Benny was so focused on the scene before him that the possibly of danger from behind was the farthest thing from his mind. After all, he could see several of the horsemen right there in front of him at the house, and he'd killed the two they'd left behind where Tommy and the boy lay dead. The rainfall that aided him in making a stealthy approach muted any audible warning he might have had too. And so it was that just as Benny was about to take his first step, he was frozen in place by a voice just a few feet behind him:

"Make one move and you're dead! I want you to drop that shotgun and then slowly unsling those rifles and drop them too. Don't turn around. Don't look back. Just do it!"

Nineteen

APRIL FELT A WAVE of relief wash over her the moment David pushed the canoe off the sand bar and handed Kimberly back to her. Afloat on the dark waters of the creek, she had the sense she really had escaped, at least temporarily, from the nightmare they were leaving behind on the farm. As she'd learned from her first time to paddle one with Mitch, a canoe would leave no tracks. The creek would take them to a place of safety, and if where they went first didn't seem far enough, they could continue downstream on the current as long as necessary.

David and Samantha paddled the canoe while she sat amidships in it with Kimberly, Lisa and Stacy paddling the other one. They were all in agreement that they should only go as far downstream as the first sandbar on the opposite side of the creek from the Henley land. It was about a quarter mile away, and difficult to reach without a boat. The men wouldn't find them there in the dark, but they would still be close enough to Mitch's usual route to and from his hunting grounds to intercept him and the guys in the morning.

"It's going to be all right, Kimberly. You're being such a good girl! We're going to have a big adventure camping out tonight, you'll see."

April knew Kimberly was confused by this sudden departure into the woods at night and in the rain at that. But she'd been through worse in the months since the collapse and was remaining surprisingly calm and agreeable. Her crying had nearly gotten them killed back in the woods by the house, but April understood how frightened she must have been at first. It was a relief that she was now going along for the ride like this was really all in fun.

It was even darker out on the creek tonight than it had been that first night out here with Mitch. With the heavy overcast preventing even starlight from penetrating the gloom, they bumped into logs and were swept by the current into overhanging branches they couldn't even see until they felt them slap against their faces. After this happened a time or two, Lisa said she was glad it was winter, and relatively cool, or else they would have the additional worry of a snake falling into the boat.

"Do you think they're looking for us now?"

"I don't know, David. It would be hard to find anybody in these woods at night, especially for people who've never been here. They probably don't even know there's a creek back here. I'll bet they'll wait until morning."

"Yeah, and besides, they're probably going through everything in the house tonight," Lisa said, the anger making her voice tremble. "They'll eat all the food we have left and take everything we own!"

"I know. I don't even want to think about it. It just makes me sick."

"Benny might stop them," David said. "If he found out they killed Tommy, he will kill all of them."

"Or die trying. That is, if he hasn't all ready. I'm worried about him."

"Yeah, me too," Samantha said. "Even if he's okay, he'll never be the same after losing Tommy like that."

April had been so preoccupied with getting Kimberly out of the house and to safety that she had not allowed herself to think too much about the fact that Tommy was actually dead. She knew it would hit her hard, probably starting now, since they were relatively safe for the moment and were still facing several hours of darkness during which she doubted she would sleep. Benny and Tommy had saved her and Kimberly from a fate she did not even want to think about. She had seen nothing but good in either of them. Both had hearts of gold and their presence at the farm had been a blessing in so many ways. Everyone there liked them and both of them were so grateful to have a place to call home after their many months of drifting up and down Black Creek, living off the land. April hoped Benny would survive this—both the risk of getting shot himself and the risk that he would simply die of a broken heart after losing both his wife and his only son in such a short period of time. She wished he were here now, with the rest of them so they could talk to him and comfort him. The reality though, if Benny was even still alive, was that he was out there in the dark rain somewhere too, no doubt looking for them while trying to elude the men who were hunting him.

The big sandbar that was their destination was easy enough to find even in the dark. When they reached it, they pulled the two canoes up to the highest level and turned them over, for shelter from the rain. It was cramped, with all five of them and Kimberly lying under the two narrow hulls, but better than sitting out in the weather all night. April just hoped dawn would come soon, and that the rain would stop when it did.

"All I wanted to do was find a Christmas tree," Stacy said. "I should have known that was stupid. We can't have Christmas again the way things are. And now we don't even have a house to put a tree in if we'd found one."

"It's not stupid," Samantha said. "There's nothing wrong with wanting to have Christmas. And we haven't lost the house yet. Don't forget that when Mitch and your brother and your cousin come back, they'll figure something out. We may have that Christmas tree anyway. It's still almost two weeks until Christmas."

"Even if we did, it wouldn't be the same without Tommy and Uncle Benny," Lisa said.

April knew she was right. Just like her dad had been right. The only thing she could count on in this life she now knew was that nothing would *ever* be the same again.

* * *

Benny did exactly as he was ordered. There was no uncertainty in the voice of the man who'd slipped up on him out of the dark, and he had no doubt that he would be dead if he made one wrong move. He opened his hand and let his beloved Remington fall to the ground beside him, and then without turning or looking back, slowly reached up first to his right shoulder and then his left to dump the slung AKs to the ground behind him. He knew there was no use berating himself for his stupidity, but it was entirely his fault. He had been so upset about Tommy and so focused on sneaking up on the house to check on the girls that he'd been careless about his own back trail. These men were more organized and more experienced than he'd given them credit for. Now at least one of them had gotten the drop on him and he had only himself to blame. But when the man spoke again, Benny knew there was more than one:

"I think Kenneth is going to be pretty happy when he sees what we've found for him, Clint."

"Yeah, it will make him feel better, I'm sure. You hear that old man? You're about to meet the father of that kid you shot in cold blood out there. What do you have to say about that?"

Benny said nothing, nor did he turn to look at his captors.

153

He just stood there in the edge of the woods and waited, until they ordered him to move forward.

"Just keep it nice and slow. We're going to walk up to the front porch. Pick up his shotgun and those AKs, P.J. And blow that horn to let Langley and Gerald know to come on to the house. They're probably still out there looking around by the road."

The man sounded the horn and Benny knew it was the one he'd heard earlier that had been a signal to the men on horseback. Benny did as he was told and walked at a deliberate pace ahead of one who was right behind him, prodding him with what he was sure was the muzzle of a rifle. He knew they'd probably kill him anyway, but it would be nice to stay alive at least long enough to learn whether April and the others had gotten out of the house or not.

"HEY DRAKE! KENNETH! LOOK WHAT WE GOT!" the man behind him shouted, when they were ten feet from the porch.

Half a dozen horses were tied up to the railing, but all the men were apparently inside until the man's announcement brought them out. Benny recognized the tall leader he'd seen earlier when he'd been watching from the woods while the horsemen waited on their signal. He hadn't gotten a good look at him then, but now he couldn't help but notice the man's wild braided beard that hung down to his upper chest. Benny figured he might have been an outlaw biker or prison inmate in the world before the collapse, or maybe he was just trying to look like a viking warrior. It made him look fierce, no doubt, but at this point Benny wasn't afraid of him or anybody else.

"Here's your shotgunner! Never would have figured he was such an old codger!" Benny's captor said. "We caught him right out there at the edge of the yard, sneaking up in the dark planning to do some more shooting. Where's Kenneth? He's gonna want to meet this fellow!"

"Kenneth's been shot bad, Clint. He's about dead. Whoever it is that's got that .22 managed to hit him with three rounds."

Benny could barely suppress a smirk at this news. So, Lisa had taken at least one of them out, and from what he gathered, he was the father of the teenaged boy he'd shot right after Tommy had been hit. If that were the case, Benny thought he might be the one who'd shot his boy. If they killed him now too, at least he would go to his grave knowing Tommy had been avenged and that they didn't know where Lisa was. Maybe April and the others were out there with her. He could only hope it was true.

The red-bearded one called Drake stepped down off the porch and walked up to Benny to get in his face. The other two that were behind him stepped forward too, and for the first time, Benny got a look at them. The one who had been speaking to him was covering him with an AR-15 suspended from a front sling at his chest. The other one had his arms full with Benny's shotgun and the two AKs he'd dropped.

155

"Who are you?" the leader asked him.

"I ain't nobody," Benny said. "Just a farmer trying to get by."

"You killed my best friend's son. That boy was only 16 years old!"

"I don't know who he was and I don't care. He shot into my herd and killed two of my steers, and whoever was with him shot my boy. Then he pulled a knife on my cowhand and was aiming to gut him with it. So yeah, I shot him. And I'd do it again too."

"You don't look like the kind of fellow that would own a place like this... all this land... this house... and cattle. What did you do, kill the owners when the lights went out and take up here like it was your own? Who's the other killer out there with the .22? Is that your other boy?"

Benny kept a stoic face as much as he wanted to breathe an audible sigh of release upon learning that these men apparently didn't even know there was a girl shooting at them. Maybe they didn't know about any of the girls... "It ain't my boy, just my other farm hand. I ain't got another boy."

"Well, you're lying to me old man. You know how I know you're lying? I know because this isn't a farmer's house. This house belonged to a game warden before the grid went down. His truck's right out back, with the glass broken out. I guess you did that to steal his issue weapon after you or one of your boys killed him, right?"

"We ain't killed anybody! My boy that died out there

156

today *was* the game warden. He was living here with me and helping me take care of the cows. With times like they are now, he hasn't been working for the state anymore. Anyone with any sense would know that."

"And you're a lying son of a bitch, old man. I saw the boy of yours that was shot out there today. Even though Kenneth split his face in two with his hawk, I didn't see any resemblance to the pictures of the man in a game warden uniform that are hanging in the office in back of the house. There are a lot of them too, and framed newspaper articles that say his name was Doug Henley. And there are pictures of his wife and his teenaged boy and girl too. Did you kill them, or did you keep the woman and the daughter alive for a while? That girl in the pictures looks like she's old enough."

Benny said nothing. It wouldn't do any good to try and keep up the ruse. They were going to do with him what they wanted to do, regardless, but now he *knew* the one called Kenneth had finished off Tommy with a tomahawk. And he had the satisfaction of knowing that Lisa had mortally wounded that same man with her rifle and that they had no idea where she was. That was good enough for Benny. He could die now if he had to, and the way things looked, he doubted there was another alternative.

157

Twenty

LISA SPENT THE ENTIRE night wide awake, her mind racing with thoughts of Tommy's death and the possibility that Uncle Benny might be dead as well while the murderous cattle rustlers were ransacking their house. Why of all nights did this have to happen—the one night that Mitch and the guys were away? They had been home every other night but two since she'd been there, and she was convinced that if they hadn't been away, those men wouldn't have gotten half as far as they did. She now second-guessed the decisions they made to turn and run to the canoes. They'd already killed two of the men creeping through the woods, and Lisa was sure she'd hit the one that opened the door. Maybe they should have made a stand or waited for the right opportunity to kill the other one too, before their friends on the horses could get there. It would have been dangerous, but maybe they wouldn't have lost the house? Now, she wondered how they would ever get it back? And she was worried about Mitch and the guys too. What if she was wrong, and they didn't pass this way on their return from the hunt? What if they simply walked into the yard in the morning, oblivious of the danger that awaited them there? They could all be killed before they knew what happened. And then what would she and April and all the others do?

These things kept her awake all night as she lay there crowded in the shelter of one of the two canoes with Stacy and April and Kimberly. As soon as it was daylight, she couldn't take it any longer. She paced back and forth on the sandbar, her .22 in hand, looking and listening for some sign of Mitch. She felt helpless and confined here, cut off from the farm and the route she expected him to take on the way home.

"I need to cross the creek," she told Stacy. "Let's put the canoe in and you can paddle me across and drop me off."

"Where are you going?" April asked.

"I'm gonna make sure we don't miss Mitch and the guys. I'm worried they're going to end up at the house unaware of what happened. I just want to get across the creek and sneak over into the woods closer to the farm. I can wait there and watch for them."

"That sounds pretty dangerous, Lisa. I'd feel better about it if I could go with you, but I can't leave Kimberly here."

"We can watch her if you want to go, April," Samantha said.

"I'll go with you, Lisa," David offered.

"No," Lisa said, cutting these ideas short before they went any further. "It will be easier for me to keep out of sight

160

alone. I know this land better than any of you. Don't worry about me, I'll be careful. All of you can still keep an eye out for the guys from here too, in case they *do* come home along the creek bank. I just want to be in position closer to the house, to make sure we don't miss them somehow. I can't stand the thought of Mitch running into an ambush."

Lisa was relieved that April and the others didn't push their objections further. Even if not for her concerns about Mitch and the guys, she didn't want to spend the morning sitting on a sandbar doing nothing. If she had to wait on their return, at least she could be doing *something*... moving around... looking... listening... It would make the time pass faster and make her feel as if she was doing her part to come up with a plan to resolve this awful situation.

She stepped out onto the opposite bank when Stacy paddled her across, and waved one time to the others before making her way up the slope and disappearing into the forest. She would work her way closer to the house, but as much as she was tempted to sneak all the way back and see what was going on there this morning, she knew that was probably too risky. Maybe, if they were lucky, the men would think the gunfight last night had frightened off whoever was living there and that they'd gone far away and wouldn't dare return. Lisa knew it was best to let them think that. Then they would be totally unprepared for what she was sure Mitch would unleash upon them when he found out what they'd done. Complete and utter surprise was a good thing. She'd seen its effects time and time again since the collapse.

She reached the thicket where the rest of the canoes were still hidden and stopped to look and listen. Something was causing her to have an uneasy feeling, but she still couldn't see or hear anything out of the ordinary. Now that the rain had stopped, however briefly, the morning woods were alive with chattering squirrels and birds. Lisa knew better than to let that lull her into a false sense of security though. Something was out there. She could feel it, and after several more minutes of watching she saw that she was right.

Three men on horseback were quietly picking their way through the trees. They were on the national forest land outside of the fence, so she knew the men had either cut the wire or they had used the other gate on the side of the property. It was startling to see them so near and she wouldn't have thought horses could move so quietly. But rain-soaked ground was on their side, and the riders were guiding their mounts at a slow, deliberate walk as they studied the muddy ground in front of them. Lisa knew they were looking for tracks, and that they'd not thought to try and cover their trail in the dark and the rain last night, and besides, there had been little time. If these men were real hunters like her dad and her brother, they would find this spot where the canoes were stashed, because five people going there on foot just hours before would have left enough of a trail. Lisa knew they were onto it, because the three men were coming right towards her. She figured her best bet would be to move laterally away from the tracks they had made last night carrying the canoes to the water. There was little time to act, so she began stepping from behind one tree trunk to the next each time all of the men were looking at the ground. By the time they'd reached the edge of the bay thicket where the boats were, she was behind a massive magnolia trunk, some 30 feet away. The men dismounted and she saw them communicating with hand signals. They were onto the trail all right, and two of them weaved and ducked into the bay trees on foot while the other waited with the horses.

Lisa was stuck, unable to move until they left, but that wasn't long, because the two that had gone in there must have quickly found the canoes. She saw them emerge quickly and then all three men climbed back into their saddles and continued on to the creek. They would see the place where the two canoes had slid into the water, she was sure. But there the trail would end. All they would know is that their quarry had fled into the creek and paddled away. Lisa hoped that would make them turn back, as it would be impossible to follow the creek bend-for-bend on horseback, even if they thought they could catch up.

* * *

Mitch was already lying awake as the first hint of daylight filtered through the trees surrounding the tarp. The morning felt colder that it really was, but Mitch knew the temperature was still well above freezing, probably in the mid-forties. With everything around them soaked it was uncomfortable and clammy, but at least the rain had stopped temporarily. He expected more to come though; that was just the way it was here this time of year when frontal systems moved across the area from the west. The rain could last two or three days or even longer, and when dry air moved in behind it, the nights probably *would* dip to around the freezing point. It was December, after all, and thinking of that, Mitch wondered how Benny and the girls had fared in their search for a Christmas tree. He hoped they found a nice one. It was a pleasant thought, celebrating the holiday as if things were almost normal, but to Mitch it wouldn't feel like Christmas no matter what they did. The thought of celebrating it without his mom and dad just made him think of them more than ever. Knowing he might never see them again ruined the spirit of it, no matter how much he might have liked to pretend otherwise.

He sat there thinking of this in silence until there was enough light to resume their search. Then he nudged Jason and Corey awake and strung his bow. When they had stretched and eaten a piece of jerky and prepared their own weapons, Mitch led the way to the area where he had a hunch they would find the deer. The rain-saturated leaves and debris on the forest floor made moving quickly without making noise effortless, even for Jason and Corey. The only disturbance made by their passage was the occasional shower of falling droplets when one of them brushed against a rain-laden branch.

Mitch wasn't looking for blood after the full night of rain, choosing instead to rely on his knowledge of the terrain and observations he'd made in the past of the behavior of wounded animals. The stricken deer would likely hole up in the thickest, most inaccessible place it could find, and Mitch knew just such a place they'd not had time to investigate before darkness overtook them the evening before. Motioning Jason and Corey to follow, he twisted his way into the dense stand of bay and palmetto and sure enough, was rewarded by the sight of Jason's fallen buck. Stone dead and already stiff, it had crawled in there and expired sometime during the long wet night. That it had suffered first, Mitch had little doubt. It was not a clean kill, but at least they'd found it so the meat would not go to waste. The cool weather would help keep it from spoiling, and they'd have it home by midmorning.

"Your kill, your job to gut him," Mitch said, looking at Jason.

"Yeah, I know. No problem. I'm just amazed you found him. I really didn't think we ever would."

"We wouldn't have given up until we did. I should have slept in and let you and Corey do it, but I didn't want to stay out here all day today."

"Yeah, I wonder why?" Corey asked with a grin.

"Really, Mitch. Tell us why? You've always been the one

who never wanted to do anything else but stay in the woods and hunt. What's changed now?" Jason laughed.

Mitch didn't mind a little good-natured ribbing from these two about April. Corey could relate to how he felt because he'd been in a relationship with Samantha for nearly a year. Jason, he was sure, had to feel left out at times. Mitch wished there was someone for him too, but who knew when he'd ever get a chance to meet a suitable girl living out here like this? And then there was Tommy, who told Mitch that he too, wanted to be married and to have a family, but that he'd always been too shy around girls to ever find one. What chance did he have of realizing that dream now, even if he could somehow overcome his inhibitions? And David was alone too, unaware that he'd once had April, the girl of Mitch's dreams.

Mitch felt a tinge of concern about Lisa and Stacy when it came to Tommy and David, especially now that both of them had recently turned fourteen and were looking more like women than girls. He had mentioned this to Jason and both agreed Tommy probably wasn't a threat, but that they should keep an eye on David, considering his mental condition and the fact that he was much closer to teenaged years himself, at only 20. For the time being though, Tommy and David seemed content hanging out with each other, having become best buddies in no time at all. Mitch would watch, but then that was his job—to watch over and protect everyone living on his family's farm.

Once Jason had eviscerated the deer, greatly reducing the weight they would have to carry, the two of them cut a small sapling as Mitch had shown them on previous hunts and lashed the animal's feet to it. They then carried it suspended upside down between them, the ends of the pole resting on their right shoulders as they walked in single-file, Corey in the front and Jason behind. It was a timeless method no doubt in use since the dawn of man. With their simple wooden bows to complete the picture, Mitch had little trouble conjuring an image of Stone Age hunters returning from the forest with sustenance for their village, the women and children awaiting them by the fires.

Twenty-one

IT WAS ALL LISA could do to refrain from stalking the three men and attempting to take them out as they sat their horses overlooking the creek and whispered in conversation. The first one would be easy, but the shot might spook the other horses before she could adjust her aim. Two would probably be doable, but three was just one too many. All of them were carrying their weapons ready for action across their saddle horns and in hand with their reins. The one who seemed to be in charge had what looked like a Winchester lever-action, but the others carried modern AR-15s or M4s with their unmistakable collapsing stocks. All three looked like tough customers, but the leader was especially scary, with his dirty-looking red beard twisted into multiple braids that hung several inches below his chin. Lisa knew that unless she could kill all three before they could react, she would be overwhelmed by their superior firepower, which she had no doubt they would unleash upon her with ruthless efficiency.

She could have picked from any of the weapons at the house that belonged to the family or among those they'd collected from dead aggressors who'd tried to harm them since the collapse, but Lisa still preferred her familiar little Ruger. She'd fired thousands of rounds through it since that Christmas four years ago when it had appeared under the tree, and it felt like a part of her. To get a sure kill with the . 22, she would have to sneak closer and shoot each man in the head or neck. It was simply too much to attempt alone, and the price of failure was too high. Once the men knew they were still facing resistance out here, all of them would be combing the woods. For all she knew, the others already were, and might arrive at any minute. She told herself the best she could do was to try and keep an eye on these three, and if they *did* decide to proceed downstream where they might see April and her other friends on the sandbar, she would take her chances and engage them then.

So she watched and waited, staying hidden behind the big magnolia, until at last the three riders turned and rode back past her and back the way they'd come. She was sure they would go back to the house and tell the rest of their gang what they'd seen. Hopefully, they had assumed everyone living here had taken to the two canoes and paddled far away. As soon as the men were out of sight, Lisa hurried back downstream to the place where she'd crossed the creek with Stacy, and called out in a whispered shout to the others waiting there. She told them what she'd seen and urged them to move the canoes into the woods behind the sandbar, so that they would be completely out of sight of anyone coming along on the bank where she was standing. Then she turned to make her way back to where she'd last seen the horsemen. She had to intercept Mitch. It was getting into midmorning now, and starting to rain again already. She couldn't imagine that he and the guys would stay out much longer in this.

* * *

Mitch moved ahead of his two friends to lead the way home, an arrow nocked on his string as always in case they jumped another deer or encountered something else unexpected. It was mid morning by the time they had worked their way back down the creek bank to the area adjacent the farm. Mitch always used a slightly different route through the area between the creek and the farm, in order to avoid making a well-trodden path others would notice. He and his father had been doing this since long before the grid went down, to keep the presence of the farm and house hidden from passerby on the creek who might happen to stop on the nearest sandbar and wander into the woods. Of course it was even more important to do so now, but even so his comings and goings brought him through the same general area, if not on a beaten path. Once they were near enough that Jason and Corey would have no trouble finding their way without him, Mitch stopped.

"You guys go on ahead. I'll be there in a bit."

"What's up?" Jason asked.

171

"Nothing. I'm just going to hit the creek for a minute; clean up a bit."

Jason and Corey laughed aloud at this. "You're gonna take a bath in the creek in this?" Corey held his hand out as if to test the air. "You're gonna freeze your ass off, Mitch!"

"He wants to smell all fresh and clean for April," Jason laughed.

"Well Samantha can just deal with it! *I'm* not taking a bath in this weather. Hell, it's not even fifty degrees!"

"There'll be a warm fire in the house when I get back," Mitch said.

"Yeah, and that's not all," Jason said.

"Go on, get out of here! You guys have got a deer to skin. I'll be there in 20 minutes!"

Mitch turned and made his way back to the bank of the creek. There was a spot near the small sandbar where they always launched the canoes that was deep enough to dive into from the clay bank just upstream. He stripped and placed his bow and arrows on top of the pile of clothes and dove without hesitation. Yes, it was cold, the water taking his breath away as it closed around him, but Mitch knew from experience that he would instantly feel warmer than he had before his dip as soon as he was back out. He had been swimming and bathing in the creek since he was old enough to walk down there, and the time of year made little difference except that he didn't linger in the water as long on days like this.

When he swam to the surface he scrubbed his scalp with his bare hands as he drifted on the current down to the sandbar, standing when he reached waist deep water again. Then he walked out, shaking his head vigorously to shake the water out of his hair, that had now reached his shoulders since the lights went out. The quick, bracing plunge was enough to make him feel great, and he would indeed be more comfortable returning to April's embrace knowing he didn't stink of sweat and the night's smoky campfire.

He had just stepped out of the water when he noticed something in the mud just four or five feet farther downstream—the keel marks made by two canoes sliding into the water. *But why in the world would anyone from the house launch the canoes now, in this weather?* The marks were fresh, only a little distorted by the rain, and Mitch quickly found many footprints in the mud farther up the bank. Several sets of tracks and the obvious marks of two boats told a story that was completely baffling. But then he noticed something else —something completely ominous and out of place here near the creek on this wet, gray morning—*the hoof prints of horses!* Mitch was already running to grab his clothes and weapons when the sharp crack of a rifle thundered through the woods in the exact direction Jason and Corey had gone!

* * *

Jason and Corey were still laughing about Mitch and his

winter bath and talking loudly when they reached the fence at the back boundary separating the Henley farm from the national forest lands surrounding it.

"How do you want to do this?" Corey asked, turning to look over his shoulder at Jason.

"Let's just set him down. You go ahead and step through and then we'll lift the bottom strand and slide him under."

Corey did as he suggested and once he was on the inside of the fence, grabbed his end of the pole again and pulled while Jason held the wire clear and pushed the buck from his side with one hand. It was almost clear and Jason was about to crawl under too when he felt a warm mist spray his face just as the report of a rifle fired from very close startled him and caused him to jerk back, snagging his jacket sleeve on the barbed wire. When he saw that Corey had fallen and realized that the splatter on his face was blood, Jason ripped his arm free and instinctively dove to the ground on his side of the wire. He abandoned his bow and quiver as a second round tore a chunk out of the fence post inches from his head. Keeping as low as possible, he squirmed on his belly to the cover of a nearby fallen log as fast as he could. As soon as he was behind it, he reached for the AR-15 slung over his back, but under the poncho he'd been wearing because of the rain. He had no idea where the rifle rounds were coming from other than somewhere on the farm side of the fence, but then he heard something big crashing through the brush beyond where Corey had fallen. When he raised his head just enough to see what it was, a man riding a black horse had appeared from the trees and stopped to aim his short cowboy-style rifle at Corey, firing it before Jason had time to react. The damned poncho was in the way and he had to yank it over his head to get the AR into action. By the time he finally did he was shaking so badly his first shot missed completely, sending the horseman wheeling around and charging off into the dense trees from where he'd appeared. Jason fired five more rounds after him, but could see nothing and had no idea if any of them connected or not. When he got to his feet, he stood there trembling with adrenalin, staring at the empty forest where the man and horse had disappeared, and at the immobile body of his cousin, Corey, whom he was certain was dead.

Twenty-two

"JASON!" MITCH TOOK IN the scene as he reached the fence and saw his friend standing there trembling, the AR-15 in his hands still pointing into the trees in the direction of the house. There had been several more shots following the first he'd heard, and he had run there as fast as he could, taking time only to pull on his pants and grab his weapons. Now he knew that Jason had fired some of those rounds, but not all of them. He saw the deer with its feet lashed to the pole lying there halfway under the bottom strand of the fence, and next to it on the other side, Corey's inert form sprawled in the grass. "What happened? Who shot Corey?"

Jason was climbing through the fence to check his cousin even as he answered. "I don't know who he was! A man on a horse! He came out of those trees over there. He shot at me too and I was trying to take cover and grab my rifle at the same time but I didn't get a chance to shoot back before he shot Corey again!"

Mitch reached the fence just as Jason recoiled in horror from what he'd seen when he knelt to see if Corey might still be alive. Half of Corey's jaw was missing and from the looks of it, and another bullet had entered his left eye socket and exited the side of his skull, leaving a gaping hole oozing bloody matter. It was a gruesome sight made exponentially worse for Jason by the fact that Corey was not only his cousin but also one of his closest friends. Mitch quickly crossed the wire to Jason's side and reached to remove the Glock 20 from Corey's belt; then picked up his bow and arrows too. Whoever did this hadn't gone far and Mitch didn't want more weapons to be available to the murderer.

"He killed him in cold blood Mitch! He sat there on his horse and just shot Corey in the head! When I got off a shot at him, I missed and then he was gone. He headed straight towards the house, Mitch, and now I'm worried about Stacy and Lisa and everybody there!"

Mitch was worried too, and with good reason. Whoever ambushed Jason and Corey was a ruthless killer who would do anything, and Mitch knew he was not alone. He could only hope the worst had not already happened. "Come on, Jason! Lets get away from this fence line before he comes back! I found the hoof prints of several horses down by the creek, so there's more than one of them, and someone launched two of the canoes too. There were tracks down there that I'm sure were made by the girls, but I didn't have time to sort it out before I heard all the shooting and ran up here as fast as I could."

Mitch was thinking hard, trying to comprehend all the

possibilities as he hurried back to where the canoes had been launched with Jason following close behind. Maybe he was wrong about who launched those boats, but he needed his moccasins and his shirt and coat anyway, so he would start there with the tracks. Things had happened so fast in just a few minutes that until now he had not even connected these events with the distant rifle shots he'd heard the afternoon before, but as he hurried back to the creek, he thought of that too. If these men had gotten there late yesterday, what had happened in the meantime? He wanted to run to the house as fast as he could to see if April and Kimberly and his little sister were there, but Mitch knew he couldn't do anything foolish. He had to force himself to be smart and careful about it, no matter how much urgency he felt. The man who'd shot Corey dead was cool and calculating, and it wouldn't help April or any of the rest of them if he got himself killed by letting his emotions get the better of him.

* * *

When Drake saw the tracks in the mud leading to the creek, and then the slide marks where two canoes had been launched, he knew they weren't going to find whoever had been living in the house easily. He also knew there were more of them that had disappeared into the woods last night than he'd first suspected. When he had gotten a look at Mosley and Hanberry in the daylight, he saw that Mosley had been shot with a high powered rifle while Hanberry had been killed with a .22, the same as Kenneth. So he'd known there had been at least two besides the old man they'd caught, but now the tracks told him there were more than that—maybe even four or five or more. They'd made their way down here during the night and escaped to the creek. With canoes to take them downstream, there was no telling how far they had already gone, and the undergrowth along the bank made it impractical to try and follow with the horses. He told Chuck and Clint as much and after discussing it for a minute, the three of them turned around to ride back to the house. Drake felt better, even if they hadn't caught whoever shot Mosley, Hanberry and Kenneth. They had the old man who'd killed his other men, and if the rest of the bunch that was living here had left by canoe, maybe they wouldn't come back at all. The best he could do right now was just to keep a sharp eye out in case they did, and then, when the rest of the people got here tomorrow or the next day, maybe he would get a posse together and go look for them. After all, there were still three canoes hidden in the woods where the two that were missing had been stashed, and they could use those if necessary.

Once they left the creek bottom, Drake told Chuck and Clint to go on to the house. "I'm gonna ride the fence line. I want to see where all my new property corners are," he said with a grin.

"We'll go with you, if you like."

"No, that's okay. Go on back to the house. I won't be long."

They were back inside the fence now, having ridden back through a side gate they'd found this morning on the east side of the house. Drake hadn't seen the rest of the cattle, but it was obvious the fence contained several hundred acres of mostly woods, so there were lots of places where the small herd could be grazing. He expected to find them soon, but the two steers Kenneth killed yesterday were more than enough to feed everybody for the immediate future. He and several of the men had ridden out there before coming down here to search for tracks and had found Marcus and Bobby dead beside the road, just as he'd expected. The old man had killed each of them with a single round of buckshot to the chest from close range. It was a damned shame, losing five good men as well as Kenneth's boy to take this place, but Drake still figured it was worth it. Aside from the excellent location and remoteness of it, the house and barn were solid. Inside the barn they'd discovered a running antique pickup and a tractor, along with extra gasoline and diesel, stored in jerry cans. There was even an old johnboat on a trailer with small two-stroke outboard mounted on its transom that Chuck said he had no doubt would run. There was also a useless newer SUV under the carport, along with the late-model game warden truck out back and a bigger state patrol boat with its fuel-injected four-stroke outboard parked in a shed. Like most of the places they had raided since the collapse, there was a mixture of the useful and the now useless. But the cattle were a big bonus, even if it was a small herd. Drake was looking forward to his first steak later in quite some time. He'd left four men out there by the road to complete the butchering of the two steers so they could bring the meat back to the house, but first the men would bury Marcus, Bobby and Kenny in shallow graves. A couple of his other guys that stayed near the house were doing the same for Kenneth, Mosley and Hanberry.

Drake had only been alone for about 15 minutes when he heard voices. He had ridden roughly back in the direction of the creek, following the fence to the lower boundary, while Clint and Chuck had gone the opposite direction, to the house. Knowing it couldn't be them he was hearing, Drake whispered quietly to his horse and walked him slowly in the direction of the sound. There was a small semi-open area with just a few scattered pines between him and the hardwood forests bordering the creek, and it was through this opening that the lower perimeter of the fence ran. The voices he heard were the voices of two men, laughing and joking about something, from the sound of it. Drake watched and waited, and seconds later he saw them, walking single-file, carrying a deer carcass on a pole between them. They looked younger than he'd expected and oddly, both of them were carrying bows and arrows instead of rifles, although he could see a large frame pistol holstered at the hip of the one in front. Drake would take that one first.

SCOTT B. WILLIAMS

He waited until they had put their weapons down and were fussing with getting the deer under the fence, then when the first one stood again on his side; he took aim at his temple and squeezed the trigger. Just as he fired his target apparently moved his head upward and back ever so slightly. The bullet hit him, but in the hinge of the jaw instead of where he'd aimed. Coming from the 16-inch barrel of his Winchester Trapper, the 240-grain jacketed hollow point .44 Magnum rounds would do a lot of damage no matter where they hit and his priority was to put the other one down before he could react. He levered another cartridge into the chamber and squeezed off another shot, but missed as his second target dove to the ground and crawled for cover. Then, Drake made a foolish mistake that nearly cost him his life. He had not seen another weapon other than the two bows and the pistol the one he'd already hit was wearing. So confident that he would catch the second one easily, he urged his horse a bit closer to finish off the first, who was still alive. His next round went through that one's eye, leaving no doubt that the job was complete.

He was about to dismount to cross the fence and go after the one that was trying to hide when he was surprised by an incoming rifle round that grazed the lapel of his jacket. He wheeled his horse to dash back into the cover of the trees and caught a glimpse out of corner of his eye of a rifle barrel over the log behind which the second one had crawled. Several more wild rounds followed the first, tearing through the foliage and ricocheting off trees around him, but somehow, he got away unscathed. Drake considered dismounting and doubling back, but not knowing whether or not there were even more than those two carrying the deer, he thought better of it and continued on to the house.

Twenty-three

LISA FELT BETTER KNOWING that April and Stacy and the others would now take the extra precaution of carrying their canoes into the woods to hide. Although she'd seen the horsemen turn back once they figured out the trail they were following led into the creek, there was no way of knowing whether or not they would return later and mount a real search up and down the banks. At least if they stayed on this side of the creek, they were unlikely to see anything. But by that time, Mitch would surely be back. She just had to find him before he went to the house.

As she crept back though the woods in the direction of the place where she'd seen the horsemen, she wondered again about Uncle Benny. If he were alive, he would probably know to come down here by the creek if he had managed to sneak up on the house and determine she and the rest of them were not inside. The more time passed without seeing or hearing anything of him, the more she worried. And when she suddenly heard two rifle shots ring out from somewhere ahead, in the area between the canoes and the farm, she wondered if the horsemen had found him. A third, single shot followed almost a full minute later, and then there were several more in quick succession, undoubtedly from a semi-automatic. Lisa felt a chill. The shooting almost had to involve the three horsemen, and who else could they be shooting at but Uncle Benny? *Unless Mitch and the guys had returned by a different route!*

She moved carefully in the direction of the gunfire, as soon as it stopped. She knew she was too far away to intervene, and she could only fear the worst: that the men had killed whoever they were shooting at and were still out there, more on edge and cautious than ever. Lisa slipped among the trees in silence as she looked for movement or sound—anything to tell her where the danger was. She saw it as she came within view of the thicket in which the canoes were hidden—just a brief glimpse through the foliage of someone walking—but enough to make her stop and raise her rifle to her shoulder. A couple more steps and whoever it was would be in view again and in her sights. Lisa waited, her finger lightly resting on the trigger of the 10/22; ready to squeeze it, when a figure emerged into the open forest at the creek bank. But what she saw was not what she expected. It was her brother, shirtless and barefoot despite the December chill, and right behind him was Jason!

"MITCH!" she called in a loud whisper.

He turned in surprise as she stepped out from among the trees where he could see her. He immediately raised a finger to his lips and pointed back in the direction from which he and Jason had appeared and she whispered again as she walked up to hug him. "Are you okay? Were those men shooting at you? Have you seen Uncle Benny? Where's Corey?"

"Corey's *dead*, Lisa! Someone shot him! What men are you talking about? Have you seen someone? Why would Uncle Benny be here? And what are you doing out here? Where is April? Is she okay?"

Her brother's questions didn't even register after Lisa heard the first words out of his mouth. *Corey was dead!* "They shot Corey? That was the shooting I just heard?"

"Yes. Someone on a horse shot him and tried to shoot Jason too."

"I have no idea who he was," Jason said. "I shot back but I don't think I hit him at all."

"I know who it was!" Lisa said. "It was one of the same men who killed Tommy yesterday. Tommy's dead, Mitch! And the men who killed him are in our house right now!"

Lisa saw the color drain from her brother's face as he took her by the shoulders and looked into her eyes. "What about April and Kimberly, Lisa? Tell me they're not dead too!"

"No, they're fine, Mitch. Everyone is okay except for Tommy, but we don't know about Uncle Benny. We haven't seen him since right after Tommy got shot."

"Where is April, Lisa? Did they all go down the creek? I

saw tracks where two of the canoes were launched."

"Yes! They're all safe. I just saw them after the three men on horses followed their trail here looking for them. I went back and told them to hide after those men turned back. I thought they had gone back to the house, but they must have still been nearby." Lisa just could not believe Corey was dead. How were they possibly going to break this news to Samantha?"

"I only saw the one guy," Jason said. "He had a long red beard and he was riding a black horse. He shot Corey with a lever-action rifle."

"I saw that one!" Lisa said. "The rifle looked like a Winchester, but the other two were carrying ARs like yours."

"Who are these people?" Mitch asked. "How many of them are there? Are there more than three?"

Lisa gave him the quick synopsis based on what she knew. She told him how it started with the shooting of the cattle. Mitch was sick when he realized he'd heard those first shots the afternoon before and dismissed them as nothing. She would never be able to convince him that he couldn't have known what was happening and that it was not his fault for not rushing back. There was no point in him beating himself up for not being there, just as Lisa realized that feeling bad for not waiting in the right place for Mitch to return wouldn't bring Corey back.

She went on to describe the shootout with the unseen rifleman that had shot Tommy, and how she'd last seen Uncle

Benny when he sent her and Stacy back to warn April and Samantha and get the travois. She told him how David had seen Tommy finished off with a hatchet and how they had all hidden in the woods and shot two of the men stalking near them in the dark woods beside the yard. She could tell Mitch was burning with rage as he listened to all this. He wouldn't stop blaming himself, not only for not coming back or for leaving in the first place, but also for not working harder to prepare better defenses to guard against just such an attack.

"Let's just go back to where April and the others are, Mitch. She's worried about you. We all were. And now we've got to tell Samantha about Corey."

"I can't right now, Lisa. I'm going to look for Benny. And, I want to see how many of these thugs we're dealing with."

"Please don't go near the house, Mitch! They know there are more of us now after seeing Jason and Corey. You might run right into an ambush!"

"I'm not going to run into an ambush. Believe me; I'll be careful."

"I'm going with you," Jason said.

"Me too, then. We'll all three go!"

"No! Neither of you are going with me! I can do this better alone. You both know that. Besides, April and everybody else must have heard that shooting. Since they know you came this way, they may be thinking it was you who got shot, Lisa. You need to get back there ASAP and let them know you're okay before they decide to come looking. You've got to tell Samantha about Corey too, but no matter what she says, you can't let her see him. None of you need to see him like that. I want you to go with Lisa and help her, Jason, because you two need to take the other three canoes and paddle them down the creek. We don't want them just waiting here for those men to use if they come back and decide to go search downstream. I'll help you launch them, and then I've got to go."

"I was thinking that," Lisa said. "They know about the other canoes. They walked right in there where they're hidden and found them."

"Take them and when you get to April, get everybody moving again and all of you go further downstream. Paddle down to the mouth of our little secret branch, Lisa. When you get there, you can pull the canoes a couple hundred yards upstream in it without leaving tracks, but I'll know where to find you when I come back. How are you set for weapons and supplies? Did you get anything out of the house?"

"We got a lot out, but we had to leave a lot of it when we ran down here after the shootout. We have some food, and a couple of blankets. We all have weapons and we brought what extra ammo we could carry: 5.56, your .357 Magnum, some 9mm and some shotgun shells. We've got more magazines for the Glocks and ARs. David's got Tommy's .308 too, and I've got all my magazines for my 10/22 and a full brick of CCI Stingers."

"Good. Give me the AR and its magazines then, Jason, and all your broadhead arrows too. You take Corey's Glock 20, but I doubt you two will need a rifle or the bow before you reach the others. I don't plan to use the rifle, but you never know. I'm taking all of Corey's arrows too, in case I get an opportunity too good to pass up."

* * *

As soon as the three canoes were at the water's edge, Mitch promised Lisa he would be careful and then he turned and set out for the road. His plan was to take a circuitous route through the heavy woods well to the east of the property boundary and the house, then cross the gravel road to the south side and work his way back west to the spot where the first shootout had taken place. There was a wooded ridge on that side of the road that would provide a natural route, and it was from approximately that area that Lisa said the first shooter had fired and hit Tommy. Mitch wanted to start there looking for any sign of Benny, knowing that if he was still alive and anywhere in the area, he would have returned there for his wounded son and found him dead.

It made Mitch sick to think that someone killed Tommy in cold blood that way. Of all the people he'd met since the breakdown of society, Benny and Tommy were the nicest and the most honest, having retained their human decency despite the tragedies they'd suffered. It was far more than Mitch

191

could say about most people. The dark side of humanity that had come to the surface as civilization unraveled was far worse than the other kind of darkness that was the direct result of the power grid failure. Mitch had seen it manifest almost immediately in the beginning, and he knew it had only gotten worse over time, especially in the more populated areas. It had reached the remote backwoods out here too, but until now not on this scale, with such a large group bent on murder and plunder finding their way all the way to the Henley farm. Mitch wondered where such a band of killers came from, and how many there were in total following the men who had forged ahead to pave the way. Lisa said that David had overheard some of them mention women and children. If it were true, Mitch figured there would probably be more men traveling with the second group as well to protect them. It would be in his best interest to do something now, while they were still divided. Maybe he could come up with a plan to take them out, but if Benny was out there somewhere, Mitch wanted to find him first. Lisa knew for sure Benny had killed one of the intruders. And she and the others had heard his shotgun twice more out by the road in the area where he was headed now. If Benny was still alive and in the fight, Mitch was sure the two of them could accomplish far more together than he could alone.

Knowing that the route he was taking was far from the house and any path that the men on horseback could use, Mitch was able to move fast. He threaded his way through an area of densely planted 10-year-old pines and reached the road at a point more than a quarter mile east of the driveway entrance. When he was sure no one was within sight of the road, he sprinted across. Closing in on the scene of Tommy's murder took much longer, as stealth was imperative. Mitch knew someone was there well before he was close enough to see. Men were talking, not especially loud, but at a normal tone as if they weren't concerned about being heard. With an arrow nocked on his bowstring and two-dozen more jammed into the soft quiver that rode close to his body so it wouldn't snag brush, Mitch crept along the ridge overlooking the road. As he drew closer, he could see that there were four men, along with two saddled horses tethered nearby. They were working at skinning the carcasses of the steers and not far away, he saw three fresh mounds of dirt, one with with a folding shovel standing upright in it by the blade. Mitch had no doubt they were graves, but whose? Lisa had told him Benny had killed the first cattle rustler there, a teenaged boy not much older than her, and Tommy had died there too, according to David. One of the graves was surely for their own fallen, but could the other two be for Tommy and Benny? It didn't seem likely that such men would bury their victims, but then again, if they planned to stay here long term, they just might. All in all, it was a mystery, but Mitch intended to have the answers soon. The men were preoccupied and still had much work to do. He would watch and make sure they were indeed alone. If so, four was not

THE FORGE OF DARKNESS

really so many with the element of surprise on his side.

Twenty-four

BENNY WAS SO TIRED he was having difficulty holding his head up. Moving to a more comfortable position was impossible, as he was sitting in one of the straight-backed wooden dining chairs from the kitchen, his hands tied behind the chair back and his ankles lashed to the wooden legs. Another length of rope was wound around his body as an additional restraint. But Benny had been surprised that they'd bothered to tie him up at all. He'd expected to be shot as soon as they were done questioning him, as he was of no real conceivable use to them. But the one called Drake, who'd asked most of the questions and who seemed to be in charge, had acquiesced when another suggested that they wait for Jimmy. Benny gathered real quickly that Jimmy was the little brother of the teenaged boy he'd shot—the one that had pulled the knife on David. And both of them were Kenneth's sons—the man who'd shot Tommy and who had died during the night of the wounds he received from Lisa's .22.

He heard them say that Jimmy ought to have his chance to get an eye for eye. "Let him do the honors," the man arguing for waiting said. "It won't make any difference to us, but it'll give little Jimmy a bit of satisfaction, getting his revenge, since he didn't get to participate in the fun here, seeing how he had to ride back and tell the others what we found. Besides that, waiting for him to get here will give the old man more time to contemplate the fact that he's gonna die for what he's done."

"Suit yourself, but just get him out of my sight and make damned sure he's tied up where he can't get loose! He's already caused me enough trouble!"

Benny had put up a fight when they grabbed him to drag him into the house. He knew it was useless, but he couldn't go out without trying. It ended when one of them kicked him so hard in the stomach that he couldn't breathe. He took a couple of hard punches to the face too, including one that had his right eye swollen shut. Now he had been tied to that chair for what he figured was nearly 12 hours. They'd put him in one of the back bedrooms, the one that had been Doug Henley's office, with the chair facing the wall. When daylight came, Benny could see with his good eye the framed pictures of the real game warden that had given away the lie he'd concocted to discourage his captors from further searching. It hadn't worked, and now Benny found himself helpless, with nothing to pass those long hours but his tortured thoughts of Tommy's death. The only thing left to look forward to now was seeing Tommy and Betsy in the next life, where Benny was certain he was headed soon.

There was nothing else he could do for his friends either, but hope they were safe. Maybe the girls had realized they needed to get far away, and maybe, just maybe, Mitch and those other two boys wouldn't come walking up into the yard before they figured out something was wrong. Benny didn't have any illusions that Mitch would be able to do anything in time to help him. With this many armed men here and his sister and his girlfriend off in the woods somewhere, taking back the house wasn't going to be his top priority, even if he knew Benny was in there. But Benny was sure he wouldn't, because nobody did other than the men who were holding him. From what he'd heard them say, there were even more of them on the road behind than there were here, including the young boy they intended to hand him over to.

They had left him alone after moving him into the office during the night, and all he could hear outside was muffled conversation and the sounds of the horses in the front yard. There was a lot of activity out there after daylight, and Benny figured they were going through everything in the house and barn, looking for anything they could use. He heard some of the men ride off on horseback, and later in the morning, he heard distant rifle shots off in the direction of the creek. The shooting had to involve his friends; he couldn't think of another explanation. The men had either found the girls where they were hiding, or they'd ambushed the boys coming back from the hunt. When he heard the door open behind him a half hour later, Benny suspected he was about to find out, and he was right. The one called Drake entered the room and jerked Benny around to face him, chair and all.

"I want to know how many of you were living here, old man! I just ran into two young men on their way back here with a deer carcass. They were both carrying bows and arrows. I guess you're going to tell me they were your 'cowhands' too, aren't you? Like anybody with a tiny herd the size of the one here would even need a hired hand…"

Benny said nothing, but he now knew the shots he'd heard had involved Mitch and the guys, rather than the girls. That didn't make it good news though, and what he heard next was even worse.

"Well if they *were* your hands, you can count yourself one short as of this morning. The other one won't be coming back, but if he does, we'll be ready for him. The son of a bitch can't shoot worth a damned, I'll tell you that. He must have fired a half a dozen rounds at me with a semi-automatic rifle, but missed every time."

Benny wasn't going to volunteer anything, so he had no way of knowing which of the young hunters was dead, or why Drake only saw two instead of all three. But he did know that Jason was the only one carrying a rifle. So that meant that it was likely Mitch or Corey. It made him sick to think about it, but he still had hope April and the girls had escaped. The thing was though, even if they had, where would they go now and how would they survive? Other than he and Tommy, Mitch and Lisa were the only ones with any real woods experience before the collapse. So if Mitch was dead, their future didn't look bright. But Benny was snapped out of his worries of the future by the back of Drake's hand striking him across his already-bruised face.

"How many?"

"The two you saw are it!" Benny said. "They're the hands I already told you about."

"No, they're not, because these two didn't know we were here. They were carrying that deer out of the woods like they were out for a Sunday stroll; laughing and cutting up, completely at ease."

"Well maybe they was going somewhere else with it then," Benny said. "Sounds like more strangers if you ask me. Lately, the place has been crawling with good-for-nothing vagrants, looking to take up where they ain't got no business!"

"Just keep being stubborn, old man. It doesn't really matter whether you answer my questions or not. The only reason you're alive now is so you can meet Little Jimmy. It'll be good for him, figuring out just what he wants to do to you before you die. It'll make him a stronger man someday. We'll hunt all your friends down like dogs no matter how many there are; so don't delude yourself into thinking you're helping them by keeping your mouth shut. It won't matter in the end."

With that, Drake shoved Benny back against the wall and left the room, slamming the door behind him. Benny's face stung from the blows, but the physical pain was nothing compared to the sadness and loss he suffered.

* * *

"Oh my God!" Stacy had whispered, when the first two rifle shots echoed through the forest, coming from exactly the direction in which Lisa had gone after warning them to hide the canoes. "They may have just shot Lisa!"

When several more shots rang out, none of which sounded like a .22. April had wished she could go and see if Lisa needed help. Maybe she'd been hit, but then again, maybe they shot so many times because they missed as she took off through the woods? It was horrible, not knowing, and also not knowing where Mitch and the guys were. She considered too that the shooting could have involved them instead, or maybe even Benny. There was no way to find out without going to investigate, but she was not leaving Kimberly to do it herself, and Stacy, Samantha, and David did not have the skills to risk stalking closer to such dangerous men in the daylight.

"As hard as it is not knowing," April said, "we've got to sit tight. We can't risk splitting up any further just yet."

"But what are we going to do if Lisa doesn't come back?" Stacy asked.

"If she's okay, she'll come back soon. If they were shooting at her, she may be hiding or running, but if they didn't hit her she'll be back. If she's not back in another hour or so, then we'll decide about looking for her."

April had her hands full keeping Kimberly quiet while they waited. A light rain was falling again, but not enough to put up with the discomfort of sheltering under the canoes as they had done all night when it rained much harder. April wished they had a tarp, but the one she'd brought from the house was with the pile of stuff they had abandoned in their haste to get out of there after the shootout. So they sat there in the wet, cool forest, she keeping Kimberly wrapped up under her poncho in her arms, while they waited and listened, their field of vision limited to just a small stretch of the creek they could make out through the trees. When something finally *did* break the monotony, it was a sound that sent a chill all the way through her—the sound of a paddle lightly banging into the side of an aluminum canoe!

April placed Kimberly under the canoe behind her and grabbed her carbine. She was almost certain the sound meant that the men Lisa had watched discuss the other canoes had returned to get them and were now hunting for them downstream. She whispered to her friends to be ready to fire as soon as the canoes came into view, but when they did, what she saw was not at all what she'd expected.

Lisa was paddling the first canoe! Behind her, Jason was paddling the second one, with a third trailing behind him on a towline. That was all of them—their entire fleet! April stepped out of the concealment of the woods to greet her and find out why they were in the canoes. And more importantly, why Jason was with her, but not Mitch and Corey? When Lisa stepped ashore and told them, Samantha let out a scream that April was sure could be heard all the way to the house. April and Stacy caught her as her knees collapsed beneath her and eased her gently to the sand as the sobs racked her body in great waves. April could not begin to imagine how she felt, and what she herself would feel if it had been Mitch instead. But from what Lisa and Jason told her of his plans, she knew she might easily find herself in the same place as Samantha later that very day.

Twenty-five

MITCH MADE A DECISION as he watched the men at work on the carcasses and determined that they were the only four out here. Attacking them from the hillside across the road could work, but would leave any he missed with an easy escape route back to the house and reinforcements. Now that he had assessed the situation, Mitch decided his best plan would be to backtrack a bit and cross the road to the same side they were on, then circle around and get between them and the house. It would be the direction from which they least expected an attack, and if any of them managed to get away, it would not be easy for them to retreat to the house. Mitch knew every possible route and he could intercept any attempt they might make to do so. He had no mercy to spare for any of these men after seeing what they did to Corey and learning of Tommy's ruthless murder. He would take out these four and whatever it took, get rid of the others that were in the house too. If more came as David had heard them mention, he would deal with them as the situation required, but that was for later. His full attention was on these four for now.

THE FORGE OF DARKNESS

Once he'd crossed the road and worked his way back around among the pines, Mitch came upon the rolling travois that Benny made from his old bicycle wheel. Lisa had told him they'd planned to move Tommy on it, but that plan changed when she learned from David that he was dead. Mitch stalked on past it and continued to close the gap on his prey. When he was close enough to hear the men talking, the conversation he overheard was music to his ears. His job was about to get a whole lot easier:

"I'm gonna go look over there in that stand of pines between here and the house and see if I can find it. I almost tripped over it last night, so I know it's there."

"If you think it's worth the trouble…"

"I know it is! That's what it's made for. They used to sell a contraption like that to haul your deer out of the woods. But I don't know who would have bought one back then, when everybody had four-wheelers for that. It'll sure make moving this beef a lot easier though. We can finish cutting it up when we get it back to the house."

Mitch knew this was an extremely lucky break. One of the men was coming his way alone to look for the travois. He would be the first to die and then there would be three— much easier to deal with all in a group than four. He carefully checked the arrow he'd selected as he waited. It was one of his best. The spares he carried from Jason and Corey's quivers would be used last, after all his favorites were exhausted.

From where he watched, Mitch was nearly a hundred feet from the other three men. If he waited until the lone man was almost upon him, the chances of the others hearing anything were very slim. Mitch had done this before, far more times than he cared to recall in the months since the lights went out, but such was the world he now inhabited. The man walking towards him looked to be about 30, his full black beard showing no gray and the rest of his face lean and tan. He carried an AK slung casually over one shoulder, clearly feeling safe on this little walk between his buddies by the road and the others that occupied the house. Mitch was low to the ground behind a dense clump of small evergreen cedars, sitting with his butt on his heels and his bow canted almost to the horizontal with the arrow resting on the upper side. He drew the arrow slowly, the motion so familiar that it was burned into his neuromuscular memory, the touching of his right thumb to the corner of his mouth telling him without conscious thought he was at full draw and ready to release the string. Mitch's target was the center of the man's Adam's apple. The razor sharp, three-bladed broadhead would cut through his throat and silence any outcry; its path out the back of his neck severing the spine if his aim was true. He let the arrow fly and saw that it was.

Mitch already had another shaft nocked and ready as the man gurgled his last breath through his own blood as it flowed onto the wet pine needles covering the ground where he'd fallen. The arrow had passed through his neck almost to the fletching, and had broken in half with a muffled snap when he fell on it. But the other three hadn't heard a thing over the sound of their ongoing chatter as they worked. They were mostly hidden from view by the trees and from where they were; they wouldn't see their fallen comrade unless they came looking for him. That was exactly what Mitch hoped would happen because it would make his task easier. He wanted to get this over with quickly and move on to the house, but he had long since developed the fine art of infinite patience when it came to hunting. Waiting would be to his advantage, so that's what he did until finally, he heard the others wondering what was taking their friend so long. They were complaining about being sick of the rain and were ready to take some of the meat back to the house to cook it.

"The hell with waiting on Gerald. He probably cut out on us went back there already," Mitch heard one say.

"If he did, I'll kick his ass when I see him."

Mitch listened to their banter until he heard enough to know that they didn't care enough to look for their buddy. They were more interested in getting back to the house with the meat, and they were ready to do it now. Mitch couldn't afford to let any of them make it back there though. He would lose the advantage he had of them being divided from the rest of their group, and besides, if they made it back there and didn't find the one he'd just killed waiting on them, it would raise an alarm. He slowly worked his way closer, getting within easy range and making sure he had clear lanes of shooting to his next targets.

He watched as they brought the two horses closer to where they'd been working to load some of the meat across the saddles. Before he moved in, Mitch had already selected three more choice arrows in addition to the one on his string, and these he held in the fingers of his bow hand, ready for quick access as soon as he loosed the first. He decided he would take the one standing there, holding the reins to the horses first, while the other two were bent to pick up their loads. The one standing also presented the most immediate danger, as he had his rifle hanging from a sling in front of his chest, while the other two had both leaned theirs against a nearby tree.

Mitch's first arrow hit the standing man in the side of the neck. The stricken man managed to take a couple of steps backwards, before almost falling on top of his two friends when he collapsed. The first of those two to turn and attempt to get to his feet was drilled through the chest by the second arrow, but before Mitch could get the third one into play and draw the bow again, the remaining man grabbed one of the AKs leaning on the tree and dove for the ground. Mitch lost sight of him momentarily, but then a wild fusillade of bullets tore into the trees around him while Mitch went to the ground himself. The man had apparently guessed the general direction from which the arrows came, but had not seen him. Now that this man's rifle fire had given away Mitch's hope of taking all four without alerting the rest at the house, he reached for his own AR and set his bow on the ground. He didn't have time to play a game of cat and mouse with this guy and it would be difficult to get him with an arrow now that he was aware of what was happening. The guy had to be freaked out, seeing his two buddies go down right beside him, pierced by silent arrows from out of nowhere. Mitch figured he would lose his nerve and either keep shooting wild or turn and make a run for it, thinking his unseen enemy was armed only with the bow. He didn't have to wait long to find out. When he saw movement again, the man had belly-crawled to the road and had just gotten to his feet to run. He was nearly out of bow range and there were branches in the way that might deflect an arrow, but he was an easy target for the AR. Mitch took aim and fired a quick double-tap, dropping him just as he probably thought he was going to get away.

Mitch knew he would run out of time fast now that there had been gunplay, so he quickly checked that the three men were indeed dead. It would have been fortunate if he could have taken one alive for questioning, but none of the three were in any condition now to discuss the circumstances of their visit here to the Henley farm. Mitch then looked around until he found Tommy's body, lying face up and partially covered with leaves. Now that he knew that Tommy wasn't in one of the three graves, he figured Benny must not be in one either. The men had apparently buried three of their own. A hurried scan of the ground in the vicinity also revealed several shotgun shell casings that Mitch was sure were Benny's. He already knew Benny had killed the boy Lisa told him about, and maybe he killed the other two buried here as well. Mitch didn't know and there was no more time to linger and speculate. At least the shell casings gave him hope that the old man *might* still be alive.

Twenty-six

"I DON'T REALLY THINK the other one will come here," Drake said, as he and Chuck discussed his encounter with the two deer hunters. Drake hadn't gotten anything out of the old man, but then he hadn't really expected to. Sure, he could have made him talk with the right application of the right kind of pain, but it was hardly worth it. The more he thought about it, the less he was worried that the one that had shot at him would dare to come here. Drake knew that whoever had been in the house before they arrived had taken to the creek in two canoes, and that meant in all probability; they had gone downstream with the current because that would be easiest. The two young men carrying the deer didn't know anything about what had happened, or they wouldn't have been walking back in the direction of the house in such a carefree manner. Drake decided that they must have been off hunting overnight and therefore had missed the other group who had left during the night in the canoes. When he had shot one of them dead, the other one returned fire when he got a chance, but seeing Drake turn his horse and gallop off in the direction of the house, he probably figured it wasn't safe to go there. If he *did* try to sneak closer to see what was going on, he wouldn't dare try anything once he saw how many saddled horses there were tied up outside.

Before he rode all the way back to the house, Drake had stopped and dismounted, watching and waiting for a good twenty minutes to see if the hunter was following him. When he saw or heard nothing, he had continued on to the house to go and question the old man.

"I imagine you're right, Drake," Chuck said. "I just don't like the thought of anybody that was living here still being alive. You never know when they might come back and try something."

"I agree, and that's why I want to hunt them all down. Unless they kept going in those canoes all the way down to the next county, it shouldn't be hard. And if they did go that far, they won't be a concern of ours."

"I wonder what's taking Clint so long. Hell, with four of them to skin and butcher those steers they should have been back grilling steaks for us all by now!"

"Yeah, well they *did* have three graves to dig first, but still…"

Drake was about to suggest that maybe they ought to send someone out there to find out what was taking so long when a series of rapid fire rifle shots rang out from that very direction.

"Uh-oh!" Chuck said. "That doesn't sound good!"

Drake threw the door open and stepped out onto the porch. One of his men had fired the shots, most likely, but at whom? Had that other fellow that shot at him managed to circle all the way out front? If he did, maybe they got him, but he wanted to know. He didn't think it was a good idea to go charging out there on the horses though, just in case. As if to prove that thought right, there were two more shots several minutes after the first series. With four of his men out there possibly engaged in hostile fire and six of their number already dead. Drake was feeling that his resources were spread a bit thin. Only six remained at the house, including him and Chuck. Maybe Clint and the others out there had whatever it was under control, but Drake didn't like the idea of not knowing and wasn't going to just sit there waiting to see.

"Chuck, let's you and I go see what's going on. We'll leave the horses here and slip out there through the woods on foot. It may be nothing, but I don't like wondering."

Before they left Drake told the four who would remain to keep a sharp watch and to split up so that two were stationed at the barn out back and two at the house. Then Drake and Chuck crossed the front yard and disappeared into the woods on the other side, taking care to avoid the lane leading to the road. Drake hoped he was doing this for nothing, and that Clint and the others would already have most of the meat cut up when they got there. But for some reason he had a bad feeling he just couldn't shake. It seemed like every time they thought they had this place under control, someone else popped up to give them grief.

Drake led the way, carrying his Winchester in one hand while Chuck had his M4, the selector switch set to 3-round burst. It was fairly easy to figure out the angle that would take them to the property corner where the steers had been killed, and the two of them soon came upon a long wooden frame with a bicycle wheel mounted on an axle at one end.

"Looks like a travois they must have built," Chuck whispered

"I think you're right. I wonder why they left it out here though?"

"Must have been planning to haul something with it and dropped it when the shooting started yesterday."

Drake figured that was it and walked on past it, making a mental note of where it was because it looked like something that would come in handy later. But he hadn't gone another 50 feet though before he spotted something else on the ground that froze him in his tracks. Chuck saw it too, and the two men spread out, moving without a sound until they were adjacent their fallen comrade. When Drake was sure they were alone, he moved closer to see what had happened to Gerald. A broken arrow protruding out of the back of his neck was the last thing he'd expected to see. Gerald's glazed and lifeless eyes stared up at the dreary gray sky above the tops of the pines, beads of rainwater dripping from his beard to mix with the pool of blood soaking the ground around his head. From the way the arrow hit him Drake figured he died instantly. He and Chuck exchanged a glance and then moved on towards the road; keeping a good twenty paces apart in case the mysterious archer was still out there waiting.

Drake struggled to wrap his mind around the fact that Gerald had been killed with an *arrow* of all things. The two young hunters he'd seen earlier had been carrying bows and arrows, and not modern compound bows, either, but the old fashioned wooden kind like the Indians used. If they had the skills to kill deer and one of his men too with weapons like that, where did they learn them? He was almost certain now that the one who'd fired at him had indeed come back and done this, and now there was nothing more important than hunting this guy down and killing him. But first he needed to talk to Clint and the others and find out why Gerald had been out in the woods alone, and whether or not they had heard or seen anything unusual. But there was only silence in the direction of the road where Clint and the rest of his crew were supposed to be.

When they reached the scene of the butchering, Drake was not completely surprised to find P.J. and Jonathan lying dead next to the two animal carcasses. The horses were standing off among the trees nearby, acting skittish like they were about to bolt at the next thing that startled them. There was no sign of Clint, but P.J. and Jonathan had both been killed the same way as Gerald—with arrows! Drake bent and studied the one that had passed through P.J.'s neck in one piece, unlike the broken one that had killed Gerald. It was without a doubt homemade, the feather fletching from a wild turkey and the broadhead a flat piece of triangular steel ground to razor edges and lashed into a notch in the other end of the wooden shaft. The archer who made the arrows was absolutely deadly with them, judging by his shot placement. Gerald and P.J. had both been hit in the neck, while Jonathan had been shot through the heart. Drake was still considering the improbability of all this when Chuck signaled him with a low whistle. He'd found Clint face down in the gravel at the edge of the road, dead of two gunshot wounds through the side of his chest.

* * *

Mitch knew the gunfire was likely to bring some of the men from the house out to investigate. As much as he would have preferred for them to be unaware he'd killed the four out by the road, he decided the diversion created by the shooting could work in his favor too. He didn't know how many might be there, but if some left to come out here, that would mean fewer to deal with when he reached the house. But he didn't want to be intercepted on the way by those that might come looking. Mitch disappeared into the woods to the east of the property, beyond the fence, and worked his way back home in another wide circle, opposite the one he'd used to get out to the road.

When he neared the open lawn, he was in back of the

house near the barn. He crept to the edge of the clearing and watched for movement. The first man he saw was obviously at a heightened state of alert. He appeared from around the corner of the barn, the AK he carried gripped like he was ready for imminent action. His gaze swept the trees at the perimeter of the yard, yet passed over Mitch without noticing him hidden among the foliage. Satisfied that all was clear, the man continued on around the barn to the shed where Mitch's dad kept his state patrol boat. Then Mitch saw another movement nearby and realized there were two of them between the house and barn. He didn't know how many more might be inside the house itself, but he figured he could take these two without anyone inside knowing it if he moved fast enough.

Slipping farther around back inside the wood line until the barn was squarely between him and the boat shed, Mitch made a silent dash across the lawn to the back wall of the structure, pressing an eye against a knothole to confirm that no one else was inside it. Then he turned the far corner and entered, crossing to shadows behind the big double gate that faced the house. He could hear the two men talking to each other, and readied four arrows in case any of his shots missed. Then he waited. They were grumbling about the rain, and complaining that it was taking forever to get the steaks they'd been dreaming about ever since they got here. Mitch listened with burning contempt. He'd show them what *forever* was! When they split up again to walk around the barn from opposite directions, he got his chance. The first one was wearing a thick jacket with a hood pulled over his head, obscuring his neck and throat, which was always Mitch's preferred target at such close range. He waited until the man faced him squarely, looking into the barn but unable to pick him out among the dark shadows within, and then he released his string to send the arrow straight into his right eye. It was a shot he wouldn't have attempted had the man not been standing completely still for that one long moment, and quite close, at some 10 yards away. But the shot was perfect and the man was dead before he hit the ground, the steel broadhead embedded deeply in his brain. Mitch exited the barn and turned the corner to the rear, creeping up behind the other one, who was completely unaware of his partner's recent demise. This one was close too, and not wearing a hood, so Mitch shot him squarely below the base of the skull, his arrow would severing the man's spine near its upper terminus and dropping him like a stone.

Knowing that any others in the house might be expecting a check-in from the two guarding the barn, Mitch quietly moved to the back of the house, crouching beneath the window that looked out from over the desk in his father's office. The blinds were open so he risked a quick look inside, raising his head to peer through the lower corner of the glass. The door to the room was shut, so he couldn't see into the hall and the living room beyond, but what he did see in the small office came as a complete and utter surprise. *Benny!*

Twenty-seven

DRAKE WASN'T SURE WHAT to make of the fact that Clint had been killed with a rifle, while his other three men had fallen to arrows. Did it mean the archer wasn't working alone, or was it that he simply carried a firearm too? If it was the same one who had shot at him earlier down by the fence, that could be the case, but that guy had been a lousy shot to miss him so many times. It made him think there must be someone else as well. Drake began to have second thoughts about the viability of his plans for this place. He'd lost ten men in less than twenty-four hours. That was just *completely* unacceptable! They had never run into this kind or resistance in a raid, especially not at a small, remote homestead like this. One thing was certain, they needed to wrap this up fast and find whoever had done all this killing before the women and children arrived, which would likely be tomorrow or early the next day. But the question was where to look? To take out Gerald and the others like that with arrows, the guy had to be like a ghost in the woods. He had gotten the drop on all of them at close range and his accuracy with his primitive weapon was simply astounding. All three had been one-shot kills, with arrow placement that would virtually guarantee instant results. Drake was nervous as he and Chuck scanned their surroundings and quietly discussed their options. It was not a good feeling, thinking they might soon become the hunted as well, the next target for those silent missiles of death flying out of the forest for their throats.

"I think we should get back to the house," Chuck whispered, after scanning the ground for tracks and finding nothing obvious. "He won't come near there."

"Maybe, but what if he does? And what if there are more of them than we think? We'd be trapped inside, making us easy targets for an attack. Whether he's alone or not, he's obviously not around here anymore, or he would have already taken a shot at us. He doesn't know we're out here and doesn't know anyone's found out what he's done yet. I say we wait a bit; keep a low profile and listen. If we hear anything from the house, we can double back fast with the two horses and maybe catch him in a crossfire between us and Langley's boys."

"Yeah, that's pretty good thinking, Drake. But damn, I've got to admit, it makes me a bit uneasy being out here not knowing, seeing how whoever it was took out four men so quickly. Clint must have been the only one that knew they were under attack before he died. The rest never saw it coming at all!"

* * *

Benny was alive! Knowing he hadn't already been gunned down was a huge relief to Mitch, but the fact that he was lashed to a chair inside his dad's office was a real dilemma. Now he had to be doubly careful to avoid giving any of the others that might be in the house a warning, because if they realized they were under attack, they might kill Benny immediately. The only reason Mitch could think of for them to be holding him was for hostage purposes. If whoever was inside there came out and found the two he'd already killed by the barn, Benny would be finished. He could hear voices and the footfalls of someone walking around inside on the wooden floors, but he couldn't tell from the sound if he was facing just two or three more adversaries or another half dozen. Ultimately, it didn't matter. He had to kill them all and cut Benny loose regardless. The only question was how to do it both quickly *and* quietly. With the men inside the walls of the house, Mitch couldn't use his arrows effectively. He had to create a diversion to draw them out, but one that would not make them think they were under attack. Mitch thought about it for a second and then came up with an idea.

He sprinted back across the space between the house and the barn and dragged the first man he'd killed around to the back of the building beside the one that had fallen there. Anyone coming from the house wouldn't be able to see them without going all the way around back of the barn, and Mitch was going to give them something else to investigate before they thought of doing that.

He went inside the barn and climbed aboard his father's ancient International tractor. Opening the tool tray inboard of the fender he took out a can of starter fluid and sprayed a little into the intake, praying the old diesel would fire right up like it usually did. The men in the house would hear it, which was exactly what he wanted. He hoped they would think that anyone trying to do them harm would never do something like starting up the tractor. He hoped they would think their two buddies did it, maybe out of boredom or curiosity. With any luck at all, they would come out here to find out.

Mitch grinned as the engine immediately came to life and smoothed to a steady rumble. He gave it enough throttle to make sufficient noise that couldn't be ignored, and then quickly ascended the ladder to the hayloft overhead. From the shadows there, he could shoot down into most of the barn's interior, so all he had to do was wait. He leaned the AR against the rough planking beside him in case something went wrong and he needed more hi-tech firepower than the longbow. It was only a few seconds after he reached the loft before Mitch heard at least two people coming out of the house talking and slamming the front door behind them. Mitch waited with his first arrow on the string until a man appeared in the barn entrance.

"What the hell? It's that old tractor, Langley!" he called back to someone who had accompanied him that was obviously waiting outside. "Tim or Richard must have started it up."

"Hurry up and shut it off! Do you see them in there? I guess they thought this would be funny!"

Perfect! Mitch thought. The running tractor had gotten the best reaction he could have hoped for. Now, he just had to kill them both and hope the two he heard talking were the only ones that had come outside. He waited until the first one reached the tractor and put his foot on the step to climb up, then he released the bowstring, sending the arrow almost straight downward into the opening just behind the clavicle at the base of the man's neck. The man collapsed with barely a sound and Mitch quickly nocked another arrow.

"What's the problem, Jennings?" the one still outside asked. "What's taking you so long?"

Mitch heard the question and knew he would only get one chance at that one. As soon he was visible in the doorway, he would see that his friend had fallen. Mitch drew the arrow to three-quarters draw, saving his muscles for the last bit until he had a target, and as soon as the man stepped into the opening, he quickly pulled to his anchor point and loosed the shaft. The arrow pierced him in the center of mass; there being little time for more exact precision. Mitch saw the look of surprise on his face as he clutched at the feathered wooden object that now protruded from his solar plexus. Mitch nocked the other shaft already in his bow hand and finished him off, shooting him a bit higher through the center of the chest, causing him to fall face forward onto the hay-littered ground. Mitch then grabbed the rifle and leapt from the loft, landing on his feet with the momentum carrying him into a deep squat. These men were no longer a threat, but this last one was lying there in plain view of the house. Mitch shut down the tractor so he could hear, then quickly dragged the body inside.

When he peeked out from the frame of the doorway, he didn't see anyone visible in the yard or on the porch. He waited another half a minute and listened, hearing nothing. Then he dashed back to the house to the spot under the window of the office, and dared another quick peek. The door to the room was still shut, and Benny was still tied to the chair there as before, slumped forward with his chin on his chest.

Mitch left his bow by the window and stepped around the corner and up onto the porch with the AR in hand. If there was anyone else inside the house, he would have to shoot, the noise be damned. It was nerve-wracking, entering the house like a SWAT-team member on a hostage rescue, but Mitch had to take the risk. He had to get Benny out of there. When no one challenged him, Mitch quickly checked all the rooms and found them empty, but for the office. His family's belongings were strewn everywhere—closets ransacked, drawers pulled out of cabinets and dumped upside down on the floor—all had been searched and pilfered from. Mitch was disgusted but at least he had the consolation that most of these low-life outlaws had paid dearly for what they'd done. He entered the office and drew his knife to cut Benny loose.

Benny was in a lot of pain, with one eye swollen shut and the circulation to his legs cut off for so long by the rope bindings that he couldn't stand on his own. When he realized what was happening, and recognized Mitch, his first words began with an apology for letting all this happen. Mitch cut him off as soon as he started:

"Benny, just stop it right now! This is *my* fault, not yours! I know about Tommy, and I am so sorry…"

"The girls?" Benny looked at him, as if he dreaded to hear the answer.

"They are okay. All of them! They're down the creek with David and Jason." Mitch didn't mention Corey. He would tell Benny about that later. "Come on. Let's get you out of here. I'll help you outside and we'll take two of those horses and head down there now. Can you ride?"

"I think so," Benny said. "But did you get all those bastards that did this?"

"I don't know. I don't know how many there were, but I can account for eight for sure. Lisa said you killed some and so did she and April."

"It was a bunch, Mitch. More than I ever would have expected to show up way out here. I just hope you got the one that was in charge. They called him Drake. Tall, hard-looking fellow with a big braided red beard like one of those *Vikings* characters."

225

THE FORGE OF DARKNESS

Mitch had not noticed all the details of those he'd killed, but he would have remembered one that fit that description, and none did. *So his work was not done...* But first, he had to get Benny to safety. After all he'd been through, he deserved to live and Mitch couldn't put him at risk for another minute.

Twenty-eight

DRAKE AND CHUCK HAD been waiting nearly a half hour and had not heard a thing, either in the surrounding woods or from the direction of the house. The mysterious archer who had killed four of his men had either gone back to where he came from or was up to something else.

"What if he's already taken out Langley and the rest at the house like he did here? He might be there now," Chuck said, growing more anxious and impatient with every passing minute.

"He may be good, but nobody's *that* good. Getting four men in the house and barn is a lot different than out here in the woods. And even out here, Clint must have managed to get off a few shots before he got hit. But you're right; we need to go see. I don't think there's any point in waiting out here any longer. But I still want to keep to the woods the way we came out here. We'll leave the horses in the trees when we get close and sneak up there on foot and take a look. I don't want to walk into an ambush!"

They doubled back on the route they'd taken to get to the

road, passing the travois along the way. Chuck tethered the two horses and they eased up the edge of the yard.

"I don't see the rest of the horses," Chuck said.

"Maybe they took them around to the barn. Let's circle around that way and have a look before we step out in the open."

When they did as Drake suggested they saw the two bodies lying in the grass behind the wooden structure. Even from a distance, Drake could see the arrow shaft protruding from the back of Richard's neck.

"That son of a bitch!" he muttered. "He did this just in the short time we've been gone?"

"I wonder where Jennings and Langley are? You think he might have gotten them too?"

"Come on. I've got to know. If I die trying to find out, then I die, but I'm going to check that house."

"I'm right behind you. Let's go!"

Drake hurriedly crossed the open lawn from the woods to the barn, and then, keeping his back to the siding, worked his way to the barn door, where he found Langley dead just inside the entrance and Jennings where he'd fallen beside the old tractor. Both died from arrows like all the rest. It was absolutely unbelievable! It was like they were up against a band of renegade Apaches from hell. Overnight, Drake and his gang had gone from being the hunters to the hunted, and now they were only two.

"We're finished here, Chuck! You and I are the only ones

left and we've lost 14 men since we found this cursed place. It's time to cut our losses and go back in time to head off the women and everybody else before they get any closer."

"I'm with you on that, Drake. It's a good thing we've still got the two horses out there in the woods. It looks like whoever did this made off with the rest."

"Yeah, it looks that way." Drake was looking around the barn, lost in thought for a second. "There's one thing I want to do before we leave, and it won't take but a few minutes. I need your help though, Chuck."

"Sure, what do you have in mind?"

Drake told him and together they began emptying the jerry cans of diesel and gasoline on the lumber and hay stacked in the back of the barn. But they saved two five gallon containers of gasoline for last, taking those to the front porch of the house and using them to douse the cypress lumber and siding, working quickly so they could do what they had in mind and be gone. Drake had hoped the old man was still tied up inside, but when he looked in through the window he saw that he was gone, the ropes that had held him in a pile beside the legs of the chair. Whoever had done the killing here had cut him loose, but there was nothing to be done about that now.

Drake had found a couple of empty soda bottles in the barn and filled them with gasoline before they poured it all out. Now he stuffed the oily rags he found in the back of the old truck into the bottles and handed one to Chuck. They lit their Molotov cocktails out in the open yard, and Chuck tossed his into the barn just as Drake's shattered on the wooden porch. The result was an instant ignition of the gasoline-soaked structures, and Drake knew that despite the light rain that was still falling, there was so much bone-dry wood under the roofs of both the house and the barn that they would burn to the ground in no time. He hadn't had much to smile about in the last few hours, but he was grinning now as the two of them ran for the woods and the horses that awaited them.

* * *

After they left the property through the gate on the east side, Mitch led the way as he and Benny rode two of the horses and led the other four that had all been tied up to the porch rail out front. Mitch had never had much interest in horses, but he had ridden a few times before the collapse with friends that kept them on their farms. The thick woods around these parts, not to mention all the fences in most rural areas of the state made horseback travel less than ideal. But once they were in the national forest beyond the fence, it was at least possible, especially since Mitch knew the area well and knew the best route to take to avoid the worst thickets and cutover.

Following the creek all the way would be out of the question, due to the vegetation, but he knew the pine ridges well enough to figure out a path to the upper reaches of the small branch where he'd asked Lisa to take the others in the canoes. He and Benny rode until they intercepted it, and then it was a simple matter of following it's course downstream until they neared Black Creek.

Not wanting to get shot because they were approaching on horseback and might be mistaken for the cattle rustlers, Mitch left Benny with the horses and covered the last quarter mile on foot, finding Lisa and all the others right where he'd hoped he would. But his gaze was locked on April and Kimberly. When Stacy noticed him and pointed his way April turned to face him and once again, Mitch knew she was the most beautiful girl he'd ever seen. She passed Kimberly over to David and leapt to her feet, practically taking him down when she ran and launched herself into his arms. Mitch felt her tears against his cheeks as he closed his eyes and squeezed her tight, neither of them speaking a word, as time seemed to stop and all that mattered for that moment was that they were together.

But when Mitch opened his eyes and looked over April's shoulder, the first sight that greeted him was poor Samantha, who had obviously fallen apart again at the sight of April's happy reunion. Lisa and Stacy were hugging her close from either side, but Mitch knew there was nothing that they, or he, or anyone else could say that would make things better for her, not now, and maybe not ever. And Benny, who had lost his beloved son, was still sitting alone back there on a horse in the woods, beaten and bruised and in need of rest and recuperation. Mitch went to get him, with April walking at his side, refusing to let him out of her sight.

* * *

Despite her protests later though, after everyone had told their stories and tried to piece together as much information as they could about the attackers, Mitch said he was going back to the house. He agreed to take one other person with him, and Lisa insisted she was the logical choice. Mitch was okay with that, as the only other he would consider was Jason. He wasn't about to leave those who stayed behind shorthanded. The chances of anyone finding them here were slim to none, but Mitch was done with discounting possibilities after all that had happened. He wanted to go back there while there was still some daylight, and if there was no sign of more of the bandits then he intended to watch the house with Lisa from the cover of the woods and see if anyone returned there after dark. It was the only way to know if they were still around, and Mitch feared they were after hearing what Benny said about the leader. Benny also confirmed what David said he'd overheard. The men they'd encountered so far were part of a larger group, and judging by what the one called Drake said when he threatened Benny, they were already on their way to the farm and not so far behind. Mitch couldn't let that happen, but he had to do more recon before he could come up with a plan.

He tore himself away from April with difficulty and he and Lisa left. Since they had the horses, Mitch figured they might as well use a couple of them, so the two of them rode quietly back along the route he'd taken with Benny earlier. They were almost to the property line when they smelled the smoke. It was heavy, and far more acrid and irritating than ordinary wood smoke from a cooking fire.

"I don't like this, Lisa. Let's leave the horses here and go the rest of the way on foot."

Mitch already had a bad feeling before they crossed the fence and entered a thick, slate gray haze of the heavy, choking smoke. It was dense enough to greatly limit their visibility, but he could find his way to the house from here by feel if he had too, and he knew Lisa could too. They finally came within sight of the house and Mitch's fears were confirmed. *The bastards had set it afire, along with the barn!*

Mitch looked for any sign of those who'd done this in his limited field of vision through the smoke, but there was no movement and nothing he could hear over the popping and hissing of the two big fires. Dark spirals of almost black smoke were spewing through several openings in the roof of the house, and under all the smoke were the raging flames that were consuming the structure and everything inside. The barn was nearly gone already, the dry hay stacked in the loft having provided more than enough fuel to create an inferno.

"Oh my God, Mitch! What are we going to do?"

THE FORGE OF DARKNESS

"There's nothing we *can* do, Lisa. It's too late! Even if there were such things anymore, a fire truck and its crew couldn't save the house now."

The fire was so hot they could barely approach the edge of the yard. Mitch and Lisa just stood there side-by-side watching, their arms around each other's shoulders, as their childhood home and place of refuge in this time of great strife was swallowed up in flames. There were so many things they needed still inside, and so many memories lost. As he stood there watching, Mitch realized that the only photo he had left of his mom and dad was the small, water-damaged and bent print he carried in a pouch in his hunting pack, having long since abandoned his wallet. It had been so long now he had mostly given up on his hopes of them returning. The two of them were likely dead and now the family home, his strongest connection to them other than his sister, was about to be no more. Everything had changed once again, and life was about to get even harder for him and those he had left.

Mitch and Lisa stayed there until nearly dark, and on the way back Lisa found the few items they had taken out the night before and later abandoned in their rush to escape. With heavy hearts the two of them mounted the horses and rode back to tell the others the bad news.

Twenty-nine

"I DON'T THINK THEY'LL be back," Mitch said, as they sat around the campfire that night, huddled on a narrow sandbar beside the clear-running waters of the branch. "They wouldn't have burned everything like that if they were planning to stay."

"It sounds to me like that Drake guy, if he's the one who did it, was really upset about losing all his men," Jason said. "Maybe he just set the fires in reaction to that, without thinking?"

"He was upset all right," Benny said, "but still, I think Mitch has a point. They didn't even get a chance to get much, if anything out of the house and barn. I figure that Drake decided to cut his losses and he won't be back. He probably went back to head off the rest of the bunch that was on their way. I wonder if he was the only one left?"

"I intend to spend some time studying tracks tomorrow," Mitch said. "I should be able to piece more of the story together. Regardless of what we think, we'll need to keep a sharp lookout. But we've got to go back there tomorrow sometime."

Mitch didn't have to say why. Everyone knew they had two graves to dig. Then, they would sort through rubble that was left and see if there was anything that could be salvaged. It was not a day he looked forward to, but if those men were truly gone and not coming back, that was almost as good as knowing he had killed every single one of them.

* * *

They buried Tommy and Corey in the side yard under the winter-bare branches of a big white oak that provided nice shade in the hot, Mississippi summers. David and Jason fashioned crosses for their grave markers from some cypress planks from the garden that had escaped the flames. Benny did his best to quote a few appropriate verses of scripture and then he said a prayer before they filled in the graves. Mitch was worried whether Samantha was going to survive this at all, but April assured him she would. She and Lisa and Stacy would give her all the attention they could and do everything in their power to help her get through. Benny was taking it hard too, but Mitch knew he wanted to live, if nothing else for those two girls who called him their "Uncle Benny." David had lost his best friend and didn't seem to know what to do with himself, but had gone to Benny and apologized for leaving Tommy when he did. Benny had admitted to Mitch that he'd been extremely bitter about that when he first figured out it happened, but when he realized David's actions probably saved the lives of all the girls; he understood it was for the best. Tommy's chances of surviving that bullet wound were slim to none anyway. He'd known that even as he sent Lisa and Stacy back to get the travois.

Sadly, that same travois had come in handy today to move Tommy's body to his final resting place, followed by Corey. When they were through with the informal funeral, Mitch and Jason used it again for the unpleasant task of moving the slain bandits off the property. There were far too many of them to bury so they took them west a good piece along the road, in the direction from which they'd come, and spent the rest of the day and that evening searching for enough dry firewood and fat lighter knot with which to burn them. The grisly sight was close enough to the road that anyone coming from that direction couldn't fail to see it. Mitch hoped such a grim warning wouldn't be needed, but he'd sent everyone else back to the place they camped the night before as a precaution. They would stay well clear of the house for the most part, until they figured out what they were going to do next.

Mitch couldn't sleep that night even long after he and Jason had returned to the campsite to rejoin the others. He was sitting by the waters edge away from the rest, staring at the current in the dark when April came and sat down beside him, asking in a low whisper if he wanted to talk.

"I was too careless, April. Way too overconfident. I

thought I was some kind of expert at this survival stuff and that I had everything figured out; everything under control."

"You *are* an expert at it Mitch. Without you, none of us would even be here now. *Nobody* has everything figured out, much less under control. You can't blame yourself for this Mitch. You know this has been going on everywhere ever since the lights went out. Those men were predators, taking advantage of the weak. They made their last mistake coming here though. You stopped them, Mitch. You drove them away."

"But at what cost? Look at us now, April. That farm with the house and the barn was the center of our universe. It was our refuge *and* our means of survival. And now we've lost it."

"You always said it was the *land* that provided what we needed, Mitch. You said it was the forest, and the creek and all the life inhabiting them. The house was shelter, but we can build shelter again. We can even build another house. What else have we got to do?"

"But it's more than just the house, April. It's all the stuff in it. My tools and other gear... the stuff I need to make more bows and arrows and everything else we need... so much of that stuff *defines* me, April! I can't imagine my life without it. Especially some of the special things Mom and Dad gave me."

"I understand how you feel Mitch, but we are *not* our stuff. It doesn't make us who we are. I know it's sad to lose those special things, but even though you lost the physical part of them, no one can take away your memories of them."

"Unless you're David," Mitch smiled for the first time since he'd sat there. "He lost you *and* the memory of ever having you!"

April pulled Mitch close and kissed him passionately. "And that's a *good* thing, because now I'm yours. We *are* going to get through this, Mitch. I'm going to help you. We'll do what we have to and we *will* survive."

"I know we will April, but everybody has got to understand it's not going to be easy. The house and barn are gone now, and I don't think we need to try and build anything back there. It was good while we had it, but like I always worried, it was also our vulnerability. Being fixed in one obvious location like that made us a target. I think going forward that we need to be more flexible, and try to stay hidden... blend into the forest... We can build shelter nearby so we still have access to what's left on the land, and keep an eye on the cattle and the horses we've just acquired, but we don't have to live on the property itself. Property lines mean nothing now anyway, and here we are, surrounded by all this national forest. I'd like to set up somewhere closer to the creek. We're going to have to redouble our hunting and gathering efforts and think about other resources we haven't been using. Benny was talking about building fish weirs and traps a while back before this happened. We can plant gardens in the spring, dispersed in several places along the creek, so they won't be easy to find. It's all going to be hard work, April, but what choice do we have?"

"I'm with you, Mitch. I never would have dreamed a year ago that I'd be living out in the country without power like a pioneer woman, but I did it. Now it looks like we're going a step further, living in the woods like wild Indians! But I can do this. I *totally* can with what you've shown me already, and I can't wait to learn more!"

"Then we get started tomorrow! We'll talk to the others about it and discuss some possible spots for our winter camp. We need to get to work on getting at least one small shelter built immediately. There will be a lot more rain coming the rest of December and probably January too. There always is. And some of the nights will be cold."

"Speaking of December, Benny and the girls never got their Christmas tree before the shooting started out there. Do you think we can still have one for them Mitch? Even if we don't have a house to put it in?"

"Of course we can! Lisa told me about the one Stacy found that Benny wouldn't cut because it was too big to get through the door. Well now it's not, because we no longer *have* a door!"

Scott B. Williams has been writing about his adventures for more than twenty-five years. His published work includes dozens of magazine articles and fifteen books, with more projects currently underway. His interest in backpacking, sea kayaking and sailing small boats to remote places led him to pursue the wilderness survival skills that he has written about in his popular survival nonfiction books such as *Bug Out: The Complete Plan for Escaping a Catastrophic Disaster Before It's Too Late*. He has also authored travel narratives such as *On Island Time: Kayaking the Caribbean*, an account of his two-year solo kayaking journey through the islands. With the release of *The Pulse* in 2012, Scott moved into writing fiction and has published seven novels with many more in the works. To learn more about his upcoming books or to contact Scott, visit his website: www.scottbwilliams.com

Made in the USA
Middletown, DE
11 August 2022